PRAISE FOR *MY SO-CALLED SUPERPOWERS*

"Heather Nuhfer has hilariously and achingly captured what it's like to be in middle school, trying to control the weird things that make you different but also super. It's impossible not to root for Veronica. **Super real, super fun, and just generally and genuinely super.**"
—Dana Simpson, *New York Times*–bestselling author of the Phoebe and Her Unicorn series

"*My So-Called Superpowers* is vibrant, lively, and hums along at a snappy pace. It has a **genuinely warm**, welcoming Saturday-morning cartoon feeling to it."
—Tony Cliff, *New York Times*–bestselling author of the Delilah Dirk series

"*My So-Called Superpowers* is a super-engaging read with plenty of action, mystery, humor, and heart. **Readers will love Veronica and her adventures!**"
—Terri Libenson, author of *Invisible Emmie* and *Positively Izzy*

Also by Heather Nuhfer

My So-Called Superpowers

My So-Called Superpowers: Mixed Emotions

My So-Called Superpowers

ALL THE FEELS

HEATHER NUHFER

ILLUSTRATIONS BY SIMINI BLOCKER

[Imprint]
MAKE YOUR MARK

New York

[Imprint]
MAKE YOUR MARK

A part of Macmillan Publishing Group, LLC
120 Broadway, New York, NY 10271

My So-Called Superpowers: All the Feels. Text copyright © 2020 by
Heather Nuhfer. Illustrations copyright © 2020 by Simini Blocker.
All rights reserved. Printed in the United States of America by
LSC Communications, Harrisonburg, Virginia.

Library of Congress Cataloging-in-Publication Data is available.

ISBN 978-1-250-13864-4 (hardcover) / ISBN 978-1-250-13865-1 (ebook)

Our books may be purchased in bulk for promotional, educational, or business use.
Please contact your local bookseller or the Macmillan Corporate and Premium
Sales Department at (800) 221-7945 ext. 5442 or by email at
MacmillanSpecialMarkets@macmillan.com.

Book design by Ellen Duda

Imprint logo designed by Amanda Spielman

First edition, 2020

1 3 5 7 9 10 8 6 4 2

mackids.com

A deadly curse entwined betwixt book and spine.
To you it will spread should your hands be caught red.

For Kate. She knows why.

CHAPTER ONE
BACK TO (UN)COOL

There were literally zero days left. The summer had zipped past like so many zippy things do: scooters, bugs, even . . . um, zippers. We stood at the precipice of The Future.

"Still here, innit?" my best friend Charlie grumbled in his faux British accent as he gazed up at the cold gray concrete face of Pearce Middle. The stark contrast between the dull building and Charlie's bright red hair strained my eyes.

"Yep," I sighed.

As usual, our lockers were in the same hall, and this year they were almost directly across from each other. It was a miracle. Charlie and I had been best friends since

1

before the dawn of time, and our lockers had never been this close. Not even when our lockers were called cubbies.

"Sweet!" I said as we both got settled.

"What's our combo again?" Charlie asked, fiddling with the lock from the set we had bought. It was tradition for us to have the same combination so we could get into each other's lockers, should the need arise. Sort of our version of the Emergency Contact you put on a field trip permission slip. Except most of the time Charlie was just borrowing books, pencils, and the occasional apple. Not that I would ever want an eaten apple returned to me.

The bell rang.

"Okay, I'm in Fisher's homeroom," Charlie reminded me.

"And I'm in McGill's."

"Ta!" Charlie raced off. His homeroom was on the next floor. Luckily mine was just a few doors down.

I casually put my hands in my pockets and fanned my fingers, wiping my damp palms on the fabric inside. I was nervous. Who isn't nervous on the first day of school? That was totally normal, but unlike all the normal kids around me, my nerves could cause a big problem. Not that long ago a very weird thing had started happening to me.

My emotions, my *strongest* emotions—you know, the ones you try really hard to hide—started showing up in real life whenever I had them. Everyone could see exactly what I was feeling! Whether I saw my crush and got bombarded by giggling cartoon hearts or shrank to the size of an ant when I was scared, my emotions could embarrass me at any moment. Not to mention all the bad stuff that would come with the world finding out what I could do. I'm not (totally) complaining, though. Over the summer I had gotten better control over my "powers," though that's a whole other messy story. Anyway, I was having fewer uncontrolled flare-ups and was even beginning to feel when my emotions were going to burst into our dimension.

Still, I was very nervous.

I slid in just as the second bell rang and took a seat in the middle of the row closest to the windows. Looking around, I saw a few familiar faces. I easily spotted Hun Su, who looked like she'd just stepped out of a cool-girl boutique's display window. She had caused me a lot of trouble last year, but we had made up over the summer when we were at film camp together. It was a lot of work but also a lot of fun, and I felt like I got to see another side of her. That side is just as perfect and beautiful, it turns out, but after spending so much time with her, I kinda felt like we came to an understanding. As much as you can really understand someone you have absolutely nothing in common with. But that was good enough for me. We shared a quick wave as Mr. McGill began roll call.

After that, it was time for announcements. The intercom crackled, and I heard the voices of two other kids from camp: the Tech Twins! Lizzie and Dean had been in charge of all things technical during our film production at camp. As you may have guessed, they were twins and very much lived up to everything TV had ever taught me about twins. It seemed like they had this psychic connection that meant they didn't need to explain anything to each other. It was super cool.

Their announcement was brief and full of info, much like the Twins themselves. They told us about the lunch offerings and team tryouts and reminded us to have a wonderful day. The Twins normally weren't big talkers, so it was fun to hear them be (forcibly) chatty. A few minutes after that, the bell rang again and I was off to art class. My absolute favorite! I looked around for Charlie. Much like our lockers had always been in the same hall, our schedules had always been the same, too. I wasn't really sure about the science of it, but I was very grateful to science, or kismet, or Mr. Gonzales, who does all the school's computer programming. Anyway, Charlie hadn't gotten there yet, so I found us an open table and got settled in. With art as my first class, I probably wouldn't be late a single day this year. Fresh from the office, Lizzie and Dean came in.

"Hey, you two!" I said once they spotted me and came over, claiming the table next to mine and Charlie's. "You did great this morning."

"Thanks," Lizzie said. "We're trying to round out our skill base."

"The goal is to be in front of the camera and behind," Dean explained.

"That's great. I love a double threat. Or a double double threat, in your case," I joked.

They both laughed.

"How's Charlie?" Dean asked.

"Good! Should be here any minute."

"Excellent," Lizzie added. "I wanted to ask him for his brother's email address."

Charlie's older brother, Nick, had run our film summer camp. I didn't have a crush on him. Never. Never ever.

The bell rang again, and there was no Charlie.

Our art teacher, Mrs. Brannon, came in and looked around the room. "Happy first day, my morning advanced artists! Looks like everyone is here," she said with a broad smile. "I'm so excited to see what each of you will come up with this term in our Free Art period."

I raised my hand and said, "Charlie isn't here yet, and I'm sure he'll want to start with us."

"Hmm." Her brow furrowed. "Well, let's get to work and see when he drifts in."

The thing is, Charlie never drifted in. Not through the whole class.

I started work on my wedding gift to Dad and Ms. Watson. I had gone through a lot of ideas trying to come up with something that would be appropriate for both of them. It had taken about three days of Charlie and me wracking our brains to conclude that no such gift existed in the entire world. My dad was a rough-and-tumble, loud, bossy, nosy, wonderful man. Ms. Watson was stiff, quiet, and exacting—like a mix of a former FBI agent and a guidance counselor, which is exactly what she was. After learning about my powers, Ms. Watson decided to protect my butt as well as be a pain in it—which I say with all the love! It's just some freaky intense opposites-attract stuff with those two. The gift I eventually landed on was a mantel-worthy portrait of the two of them, and considering realism isn't my strongest area, it was going to be a really hard project. I was just roughing out the shapes of their heads when Mrs. Brannon stopped by to see how it was going.

"I'm really pleased you're focusing on your technical skills this term, Veronica," Mrs. Brannon said.

"At least for this project," I confessed. "I think I'll always prefer more abstract art."

"What do you think about your composition there?" She pointed to the center of the canvas, between Dad's and Ms. Watson's heads.

"There isn't anything there."

"Hmm." She nodded. "Might want to consider that."

I considered it for a solid three milliseconds after she walked away. The wedding was too close and I needed to get this done. I had spent a lot of time trying to get good, natural pictures of the two of them together without seeming like I was their child stalker. I had finally decided to use one that Charlie had accidentally snapped at movie night a few weeks ago. They were both laughing, looking at the TV, but it was a great three-quarter profile shot of both of them. I was in the picture, too, sort of in the background, so I had Photoshopped myself out.

Next, I went to English class. I set one of my notebooks on the desk next to me so no one would sit there while I waited for Charlie to show up. Again, the class filled up, the bell rang, and there was no Charlie to be seen.

I pulled out my phone to text him quickly.

"This is the impression you want to give on the first day?" the voice of our English teacher boomed from over me. But that voice wasn't the kindly southern drawl of Mr. Murray. It was a pinched, commanding voice that sent shivers down my spine.

"Mr. Stephens?" I squeaked, surprised to see our drama teacher anywhere near the English rooms. Talk about drama. Mr. Stephens had never liked me. I had auditioned for every single play he put on, both at school and at the local community theater, and he never cast me. I couldn't have been that bad an actor. I mean, how bad do you have to be to get turned down for a non-speaking background role? We were also not the friendliest over the summer when my movie and his play were going to be shown at the same time. Although we found a way to work that out, our relationship had not grown even a degree warmer. Dad told me that people like Mr. Stephens thrive on creating drama, and the best thing you can do is avoid them.

"Unfortunately," Mr. Stephens told the class, "the cruise ship that Mr. Murray was voyaging on was infected with keel-to-mast dysentery. I will be subbing for him until he is feeling good again."

"Well," I corrected him before I realized I was even doing it.

"Excuse me?"

"It's, um, 'feeling well,' not 'feeling good.'"

"Correcting people is not polite, Veronica."

"I wasn't trying to be rude. It's only because we're in English class," I said meekly.

"It's always something with you," he said flatly.

Not so easy to avoid this drama, Dad, I thought.

"Which reminds me," he said, returning his attention to my attempt to text Charlie.

"Sorry," I said, and went to put the phone back in my pocket.

"Nope. Hand it over," he said, his hand stretched out directly in front of my face.

I sighed and handed him my phone. There were quite a few snickers from my lovely, mature, and supportive classmates.

"You can get it back at the end of the day," he said. Then, after he walked to the front of the room and plopped my phone into his desk drawer, he asked, "Who is missing? Did someone leave without asking permission?"

I quickly realized that Mr. Stephens was looking at the desk I had saved for Charlie. More than anything, I really did not want any more attention from Mr. Stephens. I was already embarrassed, and deep inside it felt like my powers were starting to wiggle to life. I wasn't sure how long I could control them with Mr. Stephens on my case.

"Veronica, do you have any idea? It's the seat right next to you," he asked, but I could tell he already knew.

Fighting the biggest eye roll in the history of eye rolls, I said, "It's mine. I was saving a seat for my friend."

"An imaginary friend?" he asked. The class burst out in laughter, which only egged on his theater-loving, attention-seeking ego.

"No—" I started.

"Well, there isn't anyone there, so they must not exist. Don't worry, Veronica, we'll keep your secret." He winked at the class as he pranced to the desk next to me with a few pencils and a spare calculator. After he set them meticulously on the desk, he pretended to pat the imaginary student sitting there on the head, which threw the other kids into further hysterics.

"You'll be a star pupil, I'm sure!" he said to the empty chair. It seemed as long as my classmates kept laughing, he'd keep hamming it up at my expense. "What shall we call Veronica's friend? Imagin-Amy?" he asked gleefully.

"Yes!" a few of the kids agreed.

"Great. I think it's perfect." Mr. Stephens must have noticed my silent hatred. "Oh, Veronica, don't be so serious! We're just having fun."

Yeah, fun for you. The entire class is laughing at me! I caught myself wanting to disappear. *No, no, no, Veronica,* I told myself, *do not disappear!* My stupidpowers were doing their darndest to activate. I looked down at the floor, and sure enough, my sneakers were no more than an outline. Invisibility was starting to spread up my legs. I wanted to jump up and escape! I couldn't get up. I couldn't walk out of class on nonexistent legs! I crossed them under me in hopes that no one would notice, but the invisibility was creeping up almost to my waist! Out of desperation, I flung open my

English textbook as loudly as I could, letting the hard cover of the thick book hit the desk. It made an adequately loud *BAM!* It was enough to remind Mr. Stephens that this was English class and we needed to move on.

"We'll check on our newest, most streamlined friend later," he said with a sly grin before going back to real school stuff.

So annoying. Almost as annoying as my powers. As the embarrassment wore off, the effects of my powers did, too—and I used my now-visible legs to rush out of there as soon as the bell rang.

"Bye, Veronica! Can't wait to not see you tomorrow, Imagin-Amy!" Mr. Stephens trilled after me.

I couldn't wait to vent to Charlie in our next class. But he wasn't in that class or the next one—or at lunch!

And guess what? That's how it went all day! Where the heck was Charlie?

After final period, I ran back to Mr. Murray's/ Mr. Stephens's room and retrieved my phone, somehow resisting the urge to kick him in the shin (I know, I'm a saint), and then I hurried to our lockers.

As I waited for Charlie to show up, I doodled in my notebook. My dad and his fiancée (feels super weird saying that!) were getting married in a little less than two weeks (feels even weirder saying that!), so I was just sketching out some ideas for reception decorations. My dad was a real old-timey tough guy, but he *loved* weddings. Considering how his marriage to my mother turned out, that always surprised me. Anyway, his love of the matrimonial ceremony was causing a little tension. His bride-to-be was rather insistent on a quick stop at the courthouse followed by a quiet cocktail at home.

Finally, Charlie's red head came bobbing down the hall.

"Where were you?" we asked each other at the same time.

Without another word, we both took our schedules out of our bags. I unfolded mine as Charlie tried to flatten his crumpled mess.

"Are you kidding me?" I guffawed when I saw what had happened.

"Not a single bloody class together? Veri?"

"How are we just realizing this now?"

"Well, we've never *not* had most of our classes together. And we do have a lot of the same classes," he said as he eyed the papers, "just not at the same time."

"Not cool."

"Not cool at all."

"Sup?" Betsy mumbled as she walked up to us, her black hair hanging over her eyes.

Betsy is our friend now. Betsy is our friend now. Betsy is our friend now. I often had to remind myself of this. Betsy had picked on me since kindergarten. She was bigger than everyone then and she was still bigger than me. I was never really sure why she chose me as her target, except once in fourth grade she told me my face was "very punchable." Man, things had changed in the past few months. Betsy found out about my powers and didn't tell! She was actually really cool and, more importantly, didn't find me very punchable anymore. Still, even though we had spent the remainder of the summer hanging out with her, there was something about being back in school with my former bully that made me nervous about her all over again.

"Betsy is our friend now," I blurted out.

She and Charlie raised their eyebrows at me.

"I mean, Betsy, our friend, *how* is your first day going?" I asked, then let out a tiny, awkward laugh.

"Charlie and I were gonna ask you the same question."

"'Charlie and I'?"

"Betsy and I have, like, every class together," Charlie explained. "Even health, and I'm fairly certain I'm not supposed to be in the girls' class."

"So you guys get to hang out, but I'm alone? All day? It's a conspiracy!"

"Totally!" Charlie thought for a moment before saying, "Can't you have Ms. Watson do something about that? I mean, she is a proper employee here. I'm sure she could quietly change our schedules without anyone noticing."

The three of us burst out laughing.

"Good one, Charlie," I said. "Ms. Watson bend a rule? Never!"

"Excuse me?"

We turned around to see Ms. Watson standing in the office doorway nearby.

"Did you need something from me?" she asked, her pristine black leather briefcase in her hand.

"No," we all said at once.

"I'm leaving, McGowan," she said. "Are you ready?"

"Uh, I'm going to walk with Charlie, if that's okay?" I answered.

She nodded and left.

"Ms. Watson being all over your personal life?" Betsy shuddered. "I don't know if I could ever get used to that."

"Me either. And she's about to become my stepmom."

Betsy grunted and waved goodbye as she headed to her bus.

⋆ ✶ ⋆

On our walk home, I filled Charlie in on what had happened with Mr. Stephens.

"That guy is such a drama llama," he said, just as annoyed as I was.

"I know, right?"

"I remember Betsy saying that one time she walked in on him giving an Oscar acceptance speech to the empty auditorium," he told me.

"Oh, that's so sad," I laughed. "When did she tell you that?"

"I dunno. Last week maybe?"

"You were talking over the summer?"

"She doesn't have a cell phone, but after camp we'd message when she was allowed to use her mom's boyfriend's computer," Charlie explained. "Didn't you message with her at all?"

"Uh, no, I guess I didn't really."

"She's a riot."

"I know, you may have mentioned that before. Like eighteen times," I reminded him.

"That's only because you don't listen," he teased.

"What did you say?" I joked as we got to the intersection where we each head home.

"Text me later?" Charlie asked.

"If I survive the pre-wedded bliss."

Part of my post-school routine had become heading to my dad's dental practice to meet him and Ms. Watson to get wedding stuff done. Since we were in the home-stretch now, I had expected nerves to be less frayed. I was wrong.

"It's just a few flowers," I heard my dad plead as I swung open the glass door. Its little bell let out a jingle, interrupting the bickering that had been going on.

"Kiddo!" Dad met me with a bear hug. "How was the first day?" He had already changed out of his white dentist smock and was clad in his usual uniform: black everything.

"Same old dumb stuff," I answered. "And some new dumb stuff."

"That's the spirit," he teased, and gave me an extra squeeze.

"Hey, Ms. Watson," I wheezed from my dad's enthusiastic embrace.

Ms. Watson had beat me there from school.

"McGowan, please tell your father that we don't need so many flowers. Unless we're entering the Rose Parade float contest afterward."

I giggled. Then I realized she wasn't joking.

"Flowers are nice, I think," I said with a shrug. Dad gave me a wink.

The office phone rang.

"That's the florist," Dad said excitedly as he reached for the phone. Ms. Watson smacked his hand before he could pick up the receiver.

"Hello, Melinda? Yes, he was expecting your call," Ms.

Watson said. "I know, it is a lot more flowers than we had on our original order . . ."

Dad and I cringed. She was about to throw the brake on the Flower Train. ". . . But we would still like them."

I gasped and looked at Dad. He had a cool smile on his face, but I could tell he was excited.

"Yes, it *is* very short notice. But if I could dismantle a bomb blindfolded, using only my elbows, in less than ten seconds, I think you can do this, Melinda. Thank you!"

"Wait, what?" I asked as she hung up the phone.

"Let's go get dinner, shall we?" she asked, ignoring me.

"Dinner?"

"Rik thought we could use a break from planning."

"Oh, really?" I smirked. "Or did he just know he'd be bombarding you with flowers today and would need to suck up?"

"Hmm . . . ," Watson considered as she looked at Dad. "I think it's probably wise to not think about that too much."

"Agreed," Dad added. "Sushi?"

"Yes!" I said.

* ✳ *

The walk to Dragon Roll was short, but I couldn't help noticing how crisp the air was. Summer was definitely on its way out.

"Smells like snow," I mused as I scanned the trees for any leaves that were changing color.

"It does," Dad agreed. Then he gave me a questioning look.

"It's not me," I laughed.

"Good. 'Cause if you made it snow in September, I'd have to disown you," he kidded.

My powers. Oof. Occasionally they did do some major things, but nothing that big in the past few weeks for sure. Many little bursts, but certainly not any that caused weather alerts to pop up on your phone.

When we arrived at the restaurant, I directed Ms. Watson toward the booth Dad and I usually sat in.

"Where's your father going?"

"To say hi to Sam, the owner and sushi chef. He and Dad have been friends since high school."

"That's lovely," she said, sliding into the booth seat across from me.

"And probably to tell him to make it dinner for three."

"Excuse me?"

"We just eat whatever Sam wants to make us," I explained.

"Oh, boy." Ms. Watson gulped. "I'm not sure that will work for me."

"How do you feel about sharing food? 'Cause we do that a lot. Like, *a lot*."

Ms. Watson let out three short breaths very quickly.

"You don't *have* to share with us," I offered.

"Thank you," she said genuinely.

"Happy to do a favor anytime."

"Actually, McGowan, I *was* going to ask you a favor."

"Do it!"

Ms. Watson smoothed out the paper place mat in front of her with her palms. She hesitated for a minute before she said, "I'm just going to come out and say it."

"That's probably a good plan," I encouraged her. It wasn't like Ms. Watson to be at a loss for words, which made me kinda nervous.

"It has come to my attention that I don't really have so many . . . what you might call 'girlfriends.'"

"You want to hang out with me and Betsy?" I gulped.

"No. No. Nothing like that." She shook her head. "Would you like to be my maid of honor?"

"Oh! Whoa." That was not at all what I expected to hear.

"I completely understand if your other activities would keep you from—"

"I'd love to!"

"Really?"

"Plan a bachelorette party?! Hold the big bouquet at the ceremony?! I'm down!"

"Well, I don't think we need to have a bach—"

"I'm gonna blow your mind."

"Why are we blowing minds?" Dad asked as he joined us at the booth.

"Well, Ms. Watson asked me—" I started to say, but then I saw the look on her face and felt like maybe I shouldn't say anything to Dad. She looked terrified.

"Yes?" Dad pushed.

"Oh, she asked me what my favorite type of sushi is."

"That will definitely blow your mind. This girl only eats veggie sushi."

"Say 'no' to roe, Dad."

"Ha!" Ms. Watson let out a sharp laugh that surprised us both. Luckily, we were interrupted by Sam bringing out our first course.

"Edamame and tempura for the table," Sam said as he set them down.

"Thanks, Sam!" I said. Dad dove in, but I couldn't help registering how uncomfortable Ms. Watson looked. How had I never noticed she doesn't like to share food? "Oh, Ms. Watson, do you want a separate order?"

I swear her cheeks flushed when she said, "No!" and started frantically eating the communal edamame.

"Rolls will be out soon," Sam called over his shoulder on his way back to the kitchen.

"So, what's the 'new dumb stuff' at school?" Dad asked when we were elbow deep in rice and wasabi.

"Oh, get this. Charlie and I don't have any classes together this semester! None! Zip!"

"What? That's ridiculous," Dad commiserated.

"Even worse, he has, like, all of his classes with Betsy."

"I thought you and she were pals now?" Dad asked.

"I think 'pals' is too strong of a word," I corrected him, "but she's okay."

"So, you're worried they're having all the fun without you?"

"Something like that," I said, then jammed the last piece

of my gobo-and-avocado roll into my mouth. "I gwuess its gwood to know dat pweople can change, wight?"

"Veri, chew, then speak," Dad instructed.

I had had something else brewing in the old *cabeza* for a while now, and I knew I had to ease into it.

I swallowed, then continued. "I'm just saying that we used to be really afraid of Betsy, and for good reason. She was mean to me. Like, *really* mean to me. But we worked through it and now we're friends."

"I thought she was just 'okay,'" Dad said.

"Let's not get bogged down in little details, okay? The point is that we thought Betsy was really evil and it turns out that she isn't. She just needed to be forgiven and brought into the pack with us."

Ms. Watson looked at Dad, but he didn't seem to notice.

"Well, I'm glad you are having deep thoughts and making analogies, kiddo," he said, smiling at me.

I couldn't help but notice Ms. Watson's expression. She was deep in thought and looked pretty concerned.

"What brought this on?" she asked.

"Um, was just thinking about stuff," I answered, and looked down at my empty plate.

After dinner, we walked Ms. Watson back to her car at the office. Through some mix of magic and ninja-like avoidance, I had managed not to see my dad and Ms. Watson kiss. Yet. I knew that eventually I would, but my brain just wasn't ready for it. Considering the delicate nature of my stupidpowers, I found it was best to listen to my intuition about what I could handle or, you know, I might turn into a blueberry or something.

"Question," I began as Dad and I walked home. "Is Ms. Watson ever going to move in with us?"

Dad chuckled. "Of course she is. Things have just been busy, ya know? Moving is a lot of work."

"What? Does she live in a mansion or something? If she does, we should move in there."

"She doesn't."

"Hmm. Then I'm picturing, like, a studio apartment. She doesn't seem like a person with a lot of knickknacks. Is it tiny? Why have I never been there before?"

Dad slowed down. He was searching for an answer.

I gasped, realizing why he couldn't answer me. "Wait. Wait, wait, wait. *You've* never been to her place? You're marrying someone and you don't even know if their bathroom is disgusting?!" This was madness. "Dad!"

"I know. I know!" He put his hand to his forehead. "She's just a very private person."

"What if her pantry shelves are lined with human skulls or something?"

Dad gave me his patented "Stop being ridiculous" look.

"Okay, maybe not skulls, but what if she squeezes her toothpaste out from the middle of the tube? You hate that. Possibly even more than skulls next to your canned beans."

"Well, that's what annulments are for, Veri," he joked as he unlocked the front door.

Our dog, Einstein, bounded toward us. His little white tail wagged a zillion times a minute.

"Hey, bud!" I exclaimed, picking him up. "Did you know that Ms. Watson probably has eighteen roommates?" I asked the tiny terrier. "All of them are named Steve."

"Veri, I do need to talk to you about something."

I felt my eyes go wide.

"Nothing bad," Dad reassured me. He sat on the couch and motioned for me to do the same.

"Okay . . ."

"Since we are on the topic of non-traditional marriage traditions," he began, "I was thinking you could be my best man."

I must have made a face.

"Not if you don't want to," he quickly added.

"Oh, no! I'd love to!" I told him. "It's a bit unexpected—Ms. Watson just asked me to be her maid of honor, too."

"Really? I had no idea she was going to . . . It doesn't matter. That's too much, Veri. You shouldn't do both."

"Are you kidding? There's so much fun stuff to do: I get to hold the rings and give a speech and—wait, where do I stand during the ceremony? In the middle?" My mind was racing.

"We'll figure it out. It isn't going to be a traditional wedding, kiddo. Don't go overboard."

I wasn't listening. "Oh! I get to plan the bachelor and bachelorette parties! I'm totally in!" I was so excited that my powers literally sparked and a small shower of twinkly sparkles burst from a fingertip and shimmered down onto my lap. I dusted them off and sat up straight. "I'm calm," I assured Dad.

He laughed, then said, "Let's make a list of what we

actually *want* you to do, okay? We don't need a million things going on."

"Okay, but we have to do the parties."

He thought about it for a few seconds. "Well, mine better be cooler than hers," Dad said with a wink.

"Le duh."

"Let me know if it gets to be too much."

"It won't. But I will let you know if by some nightmare situation, it becomes too much," I promised him.

I spent the rest of the evening contemplating what ideal parties for both Dad and Ms. Watson would be. Dad would want something macho and fun, but classy. Ms. Watson would want . . . what would Ms. Watson want? I was going to have to do a little digging. Maybe I should invite the other school staff? The other FBI agents who showed up when my powers destroyed the gym? Might be going too far with that last one. I needed my yearbook so I could write down the names of her school coworkers, but I was so cozy in bed, and the yearbook was all the way over on the bookshelf. I wiggled under the covers toward the end of the bed until my legs dangled off. Stretching out as far as my legs would go, I could just about hook the edge of the yearbook with my toe. "Come on," I encouraged my little piggy. With one big exhale, I caught my toe on the book's spine and flicked it out of the bookshelf! . . . Along with twenty-ish other books and a shoebox.

"Bah!" I complained as I crawled out of my comforter cocoon and slid onto the floor. I grabbed the yearbook and assessed the mess I definitely wasn't cleaning up until the next day. The toppled shoebox had a small river of pictures gushing out of it.

"I thought I got rid of you." I picked up a yellowed three-by-five photo and angled my arm to send it flying into the trash can under my desk. Then I stopped. Turning the picture toward me but still keeping it at arm's length, I couldn't help but look. My mother and baby me. Me in a baby swing. I'm smiling like crazy, but my eyes look really dark and moody. It must be the lighting, but it reminds me of how Betsy's eyes look when she's mad. Again, I was relieved that her anger wasn't directed at me anymore. Our relationship had totally changed. We were friends, which was something I never thought would happen. It made me wonder about my mom. She was afraid of me and rejected me because of my powers before, but maybe our relationship could change. Maybe there was a way she could be my mom again.

CHAPTER TWO
MESSAGE RECEIVED

"Charlie! I'm so sorry I forgot to text last night. My dad asked me to be his best man *and* Ms. Watson asked me to be her maid of honor," I explained as we walked to our lockers.

"That's fantastic!" Charlie congratulated me. "Doesn't that mean you have to do a ton of stuff?"

"Normally, yeah, but I agreed to a shorter list of responsibilities. Oh! I do get to plan some parties!"

"Your specialty!"

"Except I don't know what to do about Ms. Watson. She doesn't have . . . friends. Maybe you can help me think of something."

"Sure. I'll see what Betsy's up to," Charlie said with a smile.

"I guess. Yeah, okay." I fumbled for words as he fished a notebook out of the mess in the bottom of his locker. "I mean, did she okay your outfit choice for today?"

"That was very sassy," he answered. "I gotta roll. Lock up when you're done."

"Sure," I said, reaching to the top shelf of his locker to retrieve some gum.

"Just remember, Veri," Charlie said as he walked backward down the hall, "no one tells Charles Weathers what to wear." He went to spin himself forward but ended up tripping and landing directly in the arms of—guess who—Betsy.

"Let's go," she said, hoisting him back up. "What up, weirdo?" she called out to me.

I waved, then watched them walk down the hall. I didn't like this feeling. It *was* like Dad said. I felt like I was missing out on the fun, but it wasn't just that. Part of me wanted to end their fun. So they couldn't have any fun unless I was there. No them having fun alone together. On top of that, I could sense my stupidpowers starting to tingle. Not now! Out of the corner of my eye I spotted a green bubble wafting past me and toward the ceiling. Instantly I knew that my stupidpowers had managed to eke out one little problem. A bubble? A green bubble? What did that even mean? I couldn't reach it, but up close I could see that it was made of some kind of goo. It looked like slime. I used one of my binders to fan it out an open window. At least no one would be freaked out by seeing a bubble floating around, right?

Outside I heard a sharp *POP!* and then the surprised groan of a very irritated principal. I slammed Charlie's locker shut and clicked the lock into place before I rushed to the window and looked out. There was Mr. Chomers, covered in green slime!

Oops.

⋆ ✳ ⋆

Despite that little kerfuffle, the rest of the day was fairly uneventful. Shall I say boring? Because it was. Let's just skim a few of the high and lowlights. In that order.

Art class! Oh, how I love thee.

"Hey!" I greeted Dean and Lizzie, who were already there and opening paint.

"Portrait is already looking great," Lizzie commented as she nodded to my early sketching on the canvas.

"Oh, thanks! Wedding is in, like, a week and a half, so . . ."

"Eep!" Dean empathized.

"Event of the season!" Mrs. Brannon called from her desk.

"Guess we better invite her," I whispered to Dean and Lizzie. "Actually, that reminds me of something. Would you two be interested in documenting *the event*? And also the bachelor and ette parties? I'm going to ask Betsy to record them, but I could totally use your pro help in getting candid stuff from guests."

Lizzie and Dean looked at each other in silence for a moment before turning to me at the same time and saying, "Sure."

"Cool! Thanks!"

The period went by so fast! And I was absolutely dreading where I had to go next.

As I walked into Mr. Murray's classroom, there was more than a smattering of hushed giggles. Sitting on the desk I had saved for Charlie the day before was an open English book. Next to it was an apple with a bite taken out of it.

"Uh-oh, Veronica, I think Imagin-Amy might have stepped out on her own," Mr. Stephens said with fake concern. The kids laughed, and he mugged for them.

I didn't say anything and just walked to my desk, feeling the eyes of the other kids on me.

"This is in good fun! I hope you can see it that way. You know, grow a sense of humor!" he told me.

Yeah, right.

I made sure not to look at Mr. Stephens or the class or even in the general direction of Imagin-Amy for the entire period. I was so mad that I probably would have shot a fireball right through Mr. Stephens's overly producted hair.

*   *   *

It wasn't until final bell that I saw something that perked the day right up. It was a boy with very red hair that was now mostly covered in gross green goo. Charlie pointed at his head, a wild grin on his freshly scrubbed face.

"This was brilliant!"

"Were you with Chomers?" I asked.

"No, but we were both 'victims' of a very, very mean

practical joker, Ms. McGowan," he giggled. "Wait. You mean, you didn't leave it for me?"

"What?"

"It was in me locker. Got slimed before lunch."

I realized what had happened. There wasn't just one bubble. Another one had gone into Charlie's locker and I hadn't even noticed! Even weirder, it had hung around in the locker for all that time. My powers were usually in the moment. Once my mood passed, so did they. But not this one. It was persistent. It felt like getting a piece of food stuck between my teeth, or between me and Charlie.

"What brought that one on?" he asked, grabbing his backpack.

"Uh, I dunno. Totally rando for sure," I said quickly. "Where's Betsy?"

"She had to pick her brother up and walk him home."

"So, what else happened today? I hate not being able to talk to you . . . both."

"You mean other than getting marked? At least I look lovely in green." He paused. "It does kind of blow, doesn't it? I guess I hadn't thought about it too much."

Thanks, pal.

"What can we do?" I said. "Text?"

"No. No way. Mom said if I get busted for texting in class again, I'll be spending next summer on Uncle Mike's yam farm."

"Suggestion: Don't text *during* class."

"Impossible. It's the height of rudeness to ignore a text message. It's completely uncivilized." Charlie mimed drinking a cup of tea with his pinky finger stuck out.

"Well, then I'll just leave a bubble o' goo in your locker every day and you can figure out what it means," I joked.

"Wait!" Charlie gasped. "That could be really fun!"

"I think the powers that be might get a little suspicious if you are covered in goo every day, dude. Sorry."

"No! What if you left a superpower in my locker? It could be, like, our own secret code."

The thought tumbled through my brain. "That's still a little dangerous, don't you think? I mean, if I can even conjure up a power, I'll still have to manage it. And, you know, not burn down part of the school. Again."

Charlie had started hopping up and down excitedly. "But it would be so fun! You kinda learned how to direct your powers when we were at camp—"

"And I destroyed our movie and made everyone hate me," I interrupted him.

"But you didn't! Come on, V. Our way of communicating! *Just* ours."

It was that last little bit that hooked me.

"Okay. Okay. We can try it. It's only a trial!"

Charlie hugged me, pulling me into his bouncing. "So. Much. Fun!"

"You gotta help me figure out a party for Ms. Watson, though. That has to be part of the deal," I added. My calves were starting to cramp up.

"Sure!"

"That was quick," I said suspiciously, as our hopping died down.

"Betsy's in too!" he exclaimed.

"Good!" I said, trying to focus on the fact that I was getting what I wanted, not that everything was about Betsy.

"Why don't you come over to the house? We're sending out invitations. You could help," I offered.

Charlie shrugged.

"And Dad just got ice cream."

"Let's go!"

"You have to wash the green out of your hair here.

Dad won't handle that amount of paint in the bathroom sink. Trust me."

There were about seven thousand cards and envelopes on the dining table.

"Wouldn't it be easier to just put an ad in the newspaper?" I teased Dad, but got a stealthy nod of agreement from Ms. Watson.

"Skywriting?" Charlie offered between bites of an ice cream bar.

"Go big or go home," Dad said.

"Mrs. Brannon called it the 'event of the season,'" I told Dad.

"Well then, she gets an invitation written by me," Dad said.

"You do have very nice handwriting," I complimented him.

"We're inviting the art teacher?" Ms. Watson asked. "The art teacher we've never had any social contact with before?"

Dad reached across the table and put his hand on top

of Ms. Watson's hand. "We deserve a massive, beautiful wedding, where we can celebrate with our friends, with cake and punch and a top-of-the-line karaoke machine and dancing."

"You want a big wedding so you can justify a big karaoke party, don't you?" Ms. Watson saw right through him.

"She is good." I nudged him. And we all laughed.

"I'm doing it for the love, my dear!" Dad assured Ms. Watson, then added, "And for hits from the eighties."

There was a knock at the door.

"Enter!" Dad yelled without getting up.

"Sup," Betsy said as she walked into my kitchen.

"Betsy? What happened?"

She looked at me puzzled. "What?"

"Why are you here?" I said in the least insulting tone I could.

"I invited her," Charlie said as he closed up an envelope. "Many hands make . . . Jack a dull boy . . ." Charlie pondered. "I don't think that's right."

"He called me like twenty minutes ago," she said.

"Yeah! When I was in the WC."

"You called her from the bathroom?" I asked.

Everyone looked at him.

"I washed my hands first!" he said defensively.

"Won't you sit down, Ms. Monroe?" Ms. Watson suggested.

Betsy's eyes went wide as she looked to me, then Charlie.

"It's okay, she's nice!" Charlie reassured Betsy, and patted the seat next to his.

Hesitantly, she joined us.

"So, Betsy," Dad started, "how has your first week back been?"

She shrugged.

"I feel ya," Dad said as he slid her a stack of envelopes to stuff.

"We've actually had a lot of fun so far, haven't we, Bets?" Charlie offered. "We might even get to be partners for our social studies project."

"That'll be cool," she admitted. "Aztecs and stuff."

"Yeah," Charlie agreed.

"Well, I mean, we also have our own cool thing going on at school, don't we, Charlie?" I heard myself say.

"We do? We don't even see each other," Charlie mused.

"You know, the *thing*," I said, and made a motion with

my hand like it was a bubble that popped and dripped goo over my head.

"Oh yeah!" Charlie suddenly remembered our stupid-power messaging.

"You're not dumping anything on anyone's head, are you?" Dad asked, suspicious from my gestures.

Ms. Watson seemed to be staring at Charlie. I followed her line of sight and saw what she was really looking at: a streak of green paint just below his earlobe! I tried to gently kick Charlie under the table.

"Ow!" he shouted. "Who kicked me?"

"Sorry, it was an accident," I told him while rubbing the same spot under my ear where the paint was on him. He didn't get it, so I gave up.

"Did you check the guest list, Veri?" Dad asked. "Anyone we forgot?"

I'd been pondering something and I wasn't exactly sure how to bring it up. My gut was telling me it probably wouldn't go over very well.

"So, uh, I was thinking that maybe we should invite my mother to the wedding," I said, but it sounded a lot more like a question than I had intended.

"Absolutely not," Dad answered immediately.

"Whaaaaaat?" Charlie looked at me, aghast.

One point for my gut. "Can't we just, I don't know, invite her? Try to make things . . . copacetic?"

"Even if I knew what that word meant, I would vote no," Charlie added.

"It means to have everything in order, smooth stuff out, Chuck," Dad explained, "but there is no vote. This isn't even a thought we're entertaining."

"Of course," I muttered. "'Cause this is all about you two."

"Veri," Dad warned.

"I'm just saying. Why not? Why not give her a chance to change? For us to have a normal relationship," I complained. I could feel my powers stirring as my irritation rose, but I didn't care.

"There is nothing normal or nice about her. You know that."

"What? Are you scared?"

"Excuse you?" Dad challenged.

"Scared that I'll like her more than you."

"You know what, kiddo? I am scared. Scared that she'll drag your snotty little butt off to someone who really could hurt you. Now stop."

"You asked if there was anyone I wanted to invite." I gestured at the table. "But I guess what I want doesn't mean much anymore."

"You are being—" Dad started, but that just made me angrier.

"What am I 'being,' Dad? Oh, I forgot, it doesn't matter what I think!"

He threw his hands up in the air before taking a deep breath. "That's not true," he said in his fake calm voice.

"Pfft!" I stood up. "I'm out. You know, 'cause it doesn't matter that I'm here anyway. Do whatever you want. Invite whoever you want. Spend forever with whoever you want. Obviously, you don't need me anymore." I pushed my chair out from the table and marched toward the door.

Pfffft!!

"Oh, look!" I said, pointing at the bursts of hot steam that were shooting from each of my ears. "Great! Stupid-powers! Yet another thing I have absolutely no say in!" I slammed the kitchen door behind me.

"Well, that was awkward," I heard Betsy say through the door.

Awkward, no. Enraging, yes, I thought. But I was also already questioning myself. Why did I want to invite my

mother so badly? Why was this becoming a fixation when I had so much other stuff to think about? Fun stuff to think about! I knew one thing: I couldn't go back to the dining room. My dramatic exit had left me a little embarrassed. I needed to give all of them some time to forget it. Well, what the heck was I going to do after that? I went up to my room and crawled into bed, surrounding myself with every pillow I could find. If they were doing invitations, so would I. I did have two parties to plan, after all. I grabbed my notebook and drew a line down the center of the page. One side for Dad, one side for Ms. Watson. I quickly started writing down the names of my dad's friends: Waldo, John, Oscar, Tito, Frank—the list went on and on. Once it was time to start on Ms. Watson's side, I grabbed the yearbook and flipped to the faculty pages.

Suddenly there was a familiar clomp on the door.

"Come in, Charlie," I said. As I looked at the opening door I had to add, "And Betsy."

"All right?" Charlie asked, his brow furrowed with concern.

"Yeah, just . . . ugh." I rolled my eyes.

"So that's what it's like at your house all the time?"

Betsy asked. "You just do freaky weird stuff and no one says anything about it?"

"Pretty much."

"Cool."

"How's it looking down there?" I asked.

"Your dad mumbled something about hormones. Then Ms. Watson did something very curious," Charlie said, raising his eyebrow.

"Oh, yeah?"

"She stood up. Then sat down. Then stood up again. Then sat down again," Charlie recalled.

"Then she just went back to stuffing envelopes like a robot," Betsy added. "It was like she had a computer glitch that made her stand and sit over and over again."

"Weird," I said.

"Chuck! Your mama's calling you!" Dad shouted up the stairs.

"Does he have superpower hearing or something?" Betsy asked, amazed.

"No, that's just what he says when he wants me to leave," Charlie explained. "Be right down, Rik!"

"Suppose that means I should go, too," Betsy said.

"You really all right?" Charlie asked me.

"Yeah. Just . . . bleh."

"Lemme know if you need anything?"

"Of course. Thanks, Charlie." I felt my heart warm a little bit. My best friend was still my best friend. At least for now.

He swung the door open and held it, gesturing for Betsy to walk through. "After you, m'lady," he said in a goofy voice.

"Did you fart or something and want me to walk through it?" Betsy asked, confused.

"No," Charlie tittered nervously. "Being nice."

Betsy waved goodbye to me and walked suspiciously through the doorway. Charlie motioned for me to text him before closing the door on his way out.

What was that?!

A few seconds later, there was a crisp knock on my door. "McGowan, may I enter? I need to discuss something urgent with you."

"Uh, sure?" I answered. This was a first.

"Wow. It's very colorful in here." Ms. Watson marveled at my poster-strewn walls.

"Thanks. Are you saying the walls of your mansion are pretty bare?" I asked.

"What?" She was dumbfounded.

I sighed. "What can I help you with?"

She didn't reply.

"Ms. Watson? I thought it was urgent."

She sat on the edge of my bed, but quickly stood back up. Maybe she was malfunctioning again.

"May I?" she asked, gesturing back to the bed.

I nodded.

"It's about what happened downstairs," she started.

"Look," I said. "I probably shouldn't have gotten that upset. I didn't mean to say that about you and Dad getting married."

"That's all right. Anger is a normal emotion of adjustment. I've been reading up on these things in preparation for our next stages."

"Okay?" I had no idea what she was trying to get at.

"You could have brought up your mother any other time, but it came out rather forcefully and unexpectedly tonight."

"You're gonna have to help me out a little with this one."

"Deductive logic would tell me that you are upset about the relationship between Charlie and Betsy."

"What?!" I guffawed. Hard.

"You are displaying some very textbook symptoms.

You lashed out shortly after Betsy arrived. You seemed happy until then."

Crud. She was right.

Ms. Watson went on. "I know it is important to have a dialogue and I've read that these types of situations might be difficult for a daughter to talk about with her father."

I puffed up my cheeks with air, then pushed it out forcefully. "I am having a hard time," I said shamefully. Then my internal dam broke. The words came fast and furious: "I just didn't think . . . I mean, are they almost a couple or something? Not that that should—*would*—bother me. I don't think . . . it's . . . She was our enemy six months ago and now he's calling her 'Bets'? Bets?! And they are spending every second together and I'm just. Here. I don't know what to do. Should I do something? What could I do without looking like a desperate loner loser? I'm probably just being paranoid anyway, right? Maybe? Possibly? Perhaps?!"

Suddenly I was aware of Ms. Watson, who had gone completely stiff. Her eyes were wide and I swear she hadn't blinked in ages. Yep. I had freaked her out.

"Sorry," I said, but she was already slowly getting up.

"No. No, it's all okay," she said, but her face didn't match her calm tone.

"Once I start to vent it can be too much, I know. I forgot."

She was halfway out the door at this point.

"Oh, wait!" I said, looking at my party invite list. "Who do you want me to invite to your bachelorette party?"

"Please don't make a fuss."

"We need to make a fuss! That's the whole point," I reminded her.

"I don't want to invite anyone from my past. Really. We can skip the whole thing."

"Then what kind of maid of honor am I?" I asked.

"The kind that holds the big bouquet. Makes sure my bra strap isn't showing. The kind that has fun."

Something about that didn't work for me. "You gotta do something . . ."

"Please don't worry about it. It seems like you have enough on your plate," she said. "I'll send Rik up in a bit. I need to head home anyway."

"Nah, I'll come down with you." I hoisted myself out of my pillowy mess and followed her down the stairs, but she had basically sprinted out of sight. "See you tomorrow," I called to her. I was headed to the kitchen to intentionally miss their kiss goodbye.

"Good night, McGowan." I heard her say.

Sitting on the dining table was a massive pile of filled envelopes. They hadn't used all of them, but close to it. I grabbed one of the empty envelopes and one of the tiny blank invites and slid them both into my back pocket.

"Veri?" Dad called from the living room.

Time to face the music.

I plunked down on the couch next to him and rested my head on his shoulder.

"I'm sorry," I said.

"Not cool, you know?"

"I know. That was very rude. And childish."

"Sure was. Did you apologize?"

I cringed. "Kinda? I will tomorrow," I promised.

Dad wrapped his massive arm around my shoulders and rested his hand on the top of my head. "Things change, kiddo. Not much you can do about it. All you can control is how you react to the change."

He was right, of course, but I wasn't the only one who was going to have to accept change in relationships.

CHAPTER THREE
UNINVITED

The next morning, I got up super-duper early to go to the mall. It wasn't open yet, but I needed some specialized assistance, which I knew would be there. First, I needed to slip past the big man downstairs.

"Well, good morning," Dad said, surprised to see me up, dressed, and ready long before my alarm would normally even go off.

"Hey, morning! Heading out early today," I told him, hoping he wouldn't push.

"Where ya off to?"

Pushy Papa was alive and well.

"Uh, just some wedding stuff. Secret wedding stuff."

"Can it wait until after breakfast?"

"I believe that's why they invented to-go cups and granola bars."

"Love you," he said over his newspaper.

"Love you. Don't worry, I'll be back in time for Operation Wedding Stuff," I reassured him as I filled an insulated cup with orange juice.

"Perfect. We can't wait to listen to all of your invaluable input," he said, obviously referencing my meltdown from the day before.

I waved at him, pretending not to have heard. Dads.

It was a long bike ride to the mall, and unfortunately, it gave me a lot of time to think. As I rode, thoughts started racing through my head. What if now that Ms. Watson was around, Dad wouldn't need me to be his backup? What if I was just forgotten? And what was this whole thing with Charlie and Betsy? What if Charlie had moved on, too? As my thoughts raced, so did my anxiety. Faster and faster these scary thoughts pulsed through me until suddenly I felt the air whipping through my hair and stinging my face! Looking down, I saw that my legs were pedaling so fast that they were a blur! My stupidpowers had activated and sent me speeding impossibly fast down the road!

"Ahh!!"

I tried to slow down, but my legs had a mind of their own. All I could do was steer, and not very well. The houses whipped by as I tried to get a better idea of where I was. I was going so fast that it was hard to see!

I spotted a familiar brick corner market. State Street! I was on State Street! I needed to make a right turn soon and go into the mall parking lot the back way. But how was I going to turn at this speed without completely wiping out?! There was no way! I took a few deep breaths and tried to calm myself down. If I just stopped thinking about Dad and Watson and Charlie and Betsy I could get my powers to chill out. Problem was, the more I tried *not* thinking about my problems, the more I couldn't get them off my mind. Judging by the blur of houses, I was going even faster now than before. I had to turn. I had to stop. I had to crash. My brain took a second off from reminding me how pathetic my life was and told me a useful, if not disgusting, tidbit: It was trash day.

Ugh. I could see a pile of full garbage bags right on

the corner where I needed to turn. They were a blur, but unmistakable: big, black, grody.

"Eeeee!" I heard myself squeal as I careened into the stinky abyss. The bike stopped, but I didn't. I flew hard into the mountain of garbage.

The sound of plastic tearing and the scent of weeks-old leftovers filled the air.

"Oof," I groaned as I turned myself right-side up. My bike was lodged perfectly straight between two gigantic leaf bags. I, on the other hand, was lodged between two bags of human sadness in waste form. "Yuck." There was an open carton of moldy shrimp fried rice spread across my lap. I shook my exhausted legs free. At least my powers had worn themselves out.

After a heavy dust-off, I got back on my bike and finished the short trek to the mall. There I found a white big-rig truck parked with its back doors wide open. Standing in the opening was exactly who I was looking for.

Who woulda guessed you had to get up at the crack of dawn to sling canned cheese? I thought as I pulled up next to the delivery service entrance. Ted didn't notice me. He was deep in thought, something that was pretty common for him. He managed to keep up his zen-like demeanor and unwavering ability to speak in riddles even when he was wearing a polyester hat shaped like a dinosaur. Sure, he sold pretzels at the mall, but he was also the guy to go to when you needed something or someone. Everyone knew Ted and Ted knew everyone.

"Ted!" I called.

Ted, apparently, wasn't expecting visitors. My shout had startled him and he dropped one of the giant cans of cheese right on his foot.

"Ahh!" he cried out, cradling his mildly crushed appendage. "I mean, hi, Veronica. I mean, what are you doing here?"

"I was hoping you could help me find my mom," I said, cutting to the chase. The truck driver looked impatient.

"That don't sound like a wise to-do, little one," Ted advised, playing with his puka shell necklace.

My brain buffered for a few seconds while I decoded what he said. "I want her to get an invitation to the wedding," I explained.

Ted scratched the tip of his nose with a box of napkins. "You're telling me this is something Rik wants?"

I ignored him. "You know where she is, right?"

"I know a lot of things."

"Well, yeah, that's why I assumed you knew this, and

would help me without giving me a hard time." I paused. "Sorry. I'm cranky in the morning." I pulled the invitation out of my pocket and handed it to Ted. "Could you get this to her? It's really important to me."

He looked at me for a moment before answering, "Will do."

"Thank you!"

"What's normal is not always normal."

"Uh, okay. Thanks, Ted!"

Beep beep!

"Keep your pants on, Keith! We're learning life lessons out here!" Ted grinned at me. "Gonna be a wedding to remember."

"Yeah, I really think it will be."

I said goodbye and left Ted to his cheese unpacking. My superlegs had gotten me to the mall twenty minutes earlier than I had planned, but getting to school early actually sounded good—I could try to get some of this garbage stank off me. Plus, I could already feel my legs cramping up from their unexpected workout.

I had told Charlie I wasn't going to walk with him that day, so chances were pretty high I wouldn't see him until the end of the day. I needed to leave him a stupidmessage, but I was pretty beat. There was a familiar shape already at Charlie's locker and it wasn't Charlie.

"Hey, Betsy," I said, sidling up to her. "Can I help you with something?"

"Nah," she said as she began turning the dial on Charlie's lock. "My geography crap is in here."

I watched in disbelief. Right, left, and right she spun the dial, hitting each of the numbers.

"Charlie gave you our lock combination?" I asked.

"Yeah, well, we made it my combination, too," she said. "My locker is down by the band room, so this makes it easier."

"Oh, we do that, too. Actually, we've done that forever." It came out way snobbier than I would ever have intended.

"Cool," she said flatly. She was completely unimpressed. "You can lock up then."

Betsy grabbed her book and left. It was just me. Alone. With Charlie's locker. I had thought I was too tired to have any more powers, but I was wrong. I was starting to feel desperate that Charlie not forget me. He couldn't forget me, right? Right?!

That's when she popped into existence. On the edge of Charlie's open locker was a little me. She was about four inches tall, with about three of those inches composed entirely of head. Yes, okay, she kind of looked like a bobble-head. I checked over both my shoulders to make sure no one had seen. Then I heard a very frustrated "Hmmph!" from behind me. I whipped my head back to Lil Me. She looked very annoyed. I turned away, but she grumbled again, only louder! This time she looked at me expectantly and tapped her foot. She freaked out any time I wasn't paying attention to her! Well, that was one way to keep Charlie from forgetting me. I fished around in my backpack until I found a fun-size candy bar and gave it to her. She was so pleased that she didn't mind when I closed the door and locked her in. Now I would just have to remember to change my mood in a little bit so she would disappear. I hoped I had another little candy bar in my backpack; that could change my mood, too.

During art class I enlisted the help of Lizzie and Dean to make some party favors.

"They're called crackers," I explained. "You each pull on an end and they kinda burst open."

"Oh, yeah," Lizzie recalled, "I've heard of those. British thing."

"Something like that. Charlie introduced me to them last Christmas. Usually they're filled with toys and riddles and a little paper crown. I want to fill them with confetti and wedding-themed stuff."

Lizzie's eyes sparkled. "I think traditionally they have a little bit of gunpowder in them, so they pop when you pull them!"

"Ooh . . ." Dean shared an excited look with his sister.

"I don't think ours will."

They both groaned disapprovingly.

"Anyway," I giggled, "thanks for helping me out."

We got to work cutting rectangles of paper but were interrupted when Hun Su entered the room.

"Hello," she said to Mrs. Brannon. "Message from the office." Hun Su handed her a note. Mrs. Brannon read it and then started digging around on her desk for something that was not a paintbrush.

"Just a second . . . ," she said. "I know I have a plain old pen around here somewhere . . ."

"Hey!" Hun Su quietly greeted us as she waited.

"Hi! How's it going?" I asked her.

"It is what it is," she said cheerfully. "I probably should be asking you what you think of the news."

"News?" I asked.

"Yeah, about Charlie?" she said like she was refreshing my memory.

"Is he okay?!" A spike of fear drove through me.

"Oh, he's fine!" Hun Su said quickly.

Lizzie, Dean, and I shared a relieved look.

"I'm just talking about him and Betsy. Word on the street is that it's pretty serious."

"Does not compute," Lizzie said.

"No, I heard something about that," Dean remembered. "They're a thing, right, Veronica?"

"Uh . . . unconfirmed."

"Hmm . . ." Lizzie and Dean looked at each other.

It was awkwardly silent.

"I mean, how could they be a couple? We've only been back at school for a millisecond," I reassured myself.

"Maybe it started at camp?" Dean wondered.

"Listen. This is love. We can't question it. It's like when a pony turns into a unicorn," Hun Su said. "Magical."

"I'm not sure that's how unicorns work, mythologically," Lizzie suggested.

"Hun Su," Mrs. Brannon called her back over.

She gave us a little wave and took the note with her.

Lizzie and Dean were staring at me. Expecting something. My brain felt like a bowl of scrambled eggs, so I decided to change the subject until I had a moment to think.

"So, I'm having this problem," I started slowly until I noticed both the Tech Twins looking at me expectantly. "Ms. Watson doesn't seem to have many real friends, so I don't know what to do about her party. Who do I invite?"

"Having a party all your own? That must be fun. I'm stuck with her every stupid year," Dean teased Lizzie.

"Double the party, double the joy, dear brother."

"That's it!" I squealed.

The realization that I could combine both of the parties for Dad and Ms. Watson was such a happy revelation that I didn't even care when I got to English class and the chalkboard read, "Welcome Imagin-Amy!" I just quickly erased it before too many of my classmates could see. My brain had become laser focused, and I wanted to spend the entire period thinking about the party. Now that we were just having one party, I wouldn't have to worry about finding friends for Ms. Watson or neglecting my duties as maid of honor.

I mean, pending Dad and Ms. Watson's approval, of course.

"That sounds perfect, kiddo," Dad said.

"I appreciate the effort, McGowan, but I'm still unsure why we need all these parties," Ms. Watson reminded us.

"Because you should never turn down a party," Charlie chimed in.

We had met Dad and Ms. Watson at the Mansion House, which was exactly what it sounded like: a mansion. Not sure why it also had *house* in there. Are there mansions that aren't houses? Anyway, it was a big old Victorian mansion that was popular for weddings and, wouldn't you know it, that's exactly what we were gonna use it for.

"I think she's ready for us," Dad said to Ms. Watson, motioning at the woman who had shown us the ballroom we would be using. Dad was now worried there wasn't enough room and wanted the guests to be able to spill out into the hallway. The woman had gone to call the Mansion House's owner to see if putting chairs on the marble floors in the hallway would be acceptable. There was a little bit of tense talking, and then we overheard Ms. Watson having a moment:

"Listen, if I can affix a microchip to the bottom of a submarine in Antarctic waters while an orca is gnawing on my foot, you can sticky-pad some felt on the legs of some chairs."

"Do you think one day she'll actually tell us some of these stories?" Charlie asked.

I shrugged. "It's like she only remembers them when she's annoyed."

Charlie snorted. "Speaking of annoying, perfect supermessage today, V!"

"Lil Me hung around that long?"

"Oh, she was so done with me! She got so annoyed that she exploded and coated the walls of my locker in glitter. Looks pretty good, actually. But you must have had a really irksome day!"

I thought about what Hun Su had said in art class.

"It was definitely something."

Dad and Ms. Watson came back. Dad had a big smile on his face.

"All settled!" he said.

"And you're sure John is properly certified to marry us?" Ms. Watson asked him.

"Yes. It's totally legit. He did the online certification thingy," Dad said, trying to reassure her. It didn't really work.

"I'd like to see that paperwork."

"Ms. Watson," Charlie started as we walked to the car, "what were you saying about a submarine?"

"Well, Charles, if I told you that story, I'd have to kill you."

Charlie laughed. Ms. Watson didn't.

CHAPTER FOUR

LET THEM EAT CAKE. ALL THE CAKE.

It was Saturday. A very important day in the world of wedding prep. With only a week to go until the big day, the scramble was on! But there would be no scrambling today. At least not in a literal sense. There would be only chomping.

"Cake day!" Charlie bellowed happily when he opened his front door.

"Cake day!" I echoed. "You ready?"

"I was born ready for cake day."

Somehow Charlie had convinced Dad that he needed to come with us when we did taste testing on wedding cakes. We turned back toward the driveway, where Dad and Ms. Watson were waiting in the car. Dad rolled down his window.

"Got a jacket there, bud?"

Charlie stopped in his tracks.

"The cake will keep me warm," he insisted.

Dad motioned for Charlie to go back in the house. I went with him. There wasn't a lot of fun to be had in the car, and besides, it was always nice to see Charlie's moms. They were both unbelievably smart scientists who tried to help me with my powers. His mom Lucia was one of the nicest people I'd ever met, and his other mom, Dr. Weathers, was pretty cool, too, even if you did have to call her "Dr. Weathers."

Lucia was in the entryway when we went back in. Charlie flew up the stairs to his room.

"Veronica!" She greeted me before wrapping me in a hug.

"Hi! Just grabbing Charlie a jacket before—"

"Cake day!" she laughed.

"Yeah," I giggled.

There was a muffled crashing noise upstairs.

"I'm fine!" Charlie called down.

"This might take a while." Lucia motioned for me to

sit down on the sofa while we waited. "You know we are trying to get Charlie to take better care of his things, so I had to stop helping him find stuff." She twisted her hands. It was obviously hard for her.

I tried to take her mind off of it. "He can be really good at finding things. One time I couldn't find one of my sketching pencils for hours and Charlie found it right away."

"Where was it?"

"In my hair," I confessed.

She covered her chuckle. I liked talking to Lucia. There was something about her that made me feel comfortable saying anything.

"Well, it's not the weirdest thing he's seen from me, so . . . ," I joked.

Lucia sat up straighter. A flicker of recognition swept across her face. "How have you been doing? Your abilities, I mean."

"Pretty low-grade lately," I told her. Then I remembered Lil Me and paint balloons . . . and the invisibility . . . and the steam ears. "Kinda."

"Do you think they're diminishing?"

"Oh gosh no," I said instantly.

"And how are you feeling about them?"

"Not my favorite thing, to be honest," I answered. "They're better than they were . . . sometimes. And I've gotten kinda used to them . . . maybe. But if I had a magic wand . . ."

"You would make it so you didn't have the powers at all?"

"Absolutely," I said. I didn't think about it for even a millisecond.

"Great!" Lucia's eyes lit up.

"Argh!" Charlie huffed from upstairs. It sounded like he was having a hard time with something.

SLAM! Charlie's bedroom door shut. He clomped down the stairs at record speed.

"Ready!" He was wearing a dark purple zip-front hoodie that was as wrinkled as last week's lunch bag. "Cake day awaits!" Charlie grabbed my arm and whisked me toward the door. "Bye, mum! Love you!"

The slam of the front door cut through the air before I could even say my goodbye.

"Uh-oh, Parental Smooch Alert, Veri," Charlie warned me as we approached the car.

I averted my eyes, suddenly taking an intense interest

in the mulch that lined Charlie's driveway as I got into the car.

"Thanks again for inviting me, Rik!" Charlie said as we drove toward town.

"My pleasure, Chuck. The more of *their* cake you eat, the less of *my* groceries you eat."

Fast-forward to thirty minutes later: Two of us were ready to never eat cake again. The other two, on the other hand . . .

"Why not get all of them?" Charlie asked between bites of cake.

"Now that's a good idea," Dad agreed as he shoved another fork load of chocolate layer cake into his mouth.

Ms. Watson and I shared a pained look.

"I really quite liked the cinnamon," Ms. Watson offered, "but I wasn't fond of the frosting. The chocolate frosting on the raspberry cake was good."

"The cinnamon is a good autumnal flavor," I agreed. "Oh, wait! What if you got the Mexican chocolate frosting on the cinnamon cake as one layer . . ."

Charlie's jaw dropped, revealing half-eaten marble cake. "Yes."

"And then the second could be the caramel cake with buttercream?"

"Sign me up!" Dad agreed.

"Then the top could be something that is, like, each of your favorites. Since that will be the one you keep to eat on your anniversary."

"You keep a cake for a whole year?" Ms. Watson asked.

"In the freezer," I reassured her. I'd done my research.

I looked at Ms. Watson. I could tell by the faraway expression in her eyes that she was struggling with the thought of eating cake old enough to have a birthday. Dad could tell, too.

"You can never have too much cake."

"Truer words were never spoken," Charlie agreed.

The baker interrupted the massive cake plea. "Eight flavors down. Any favorites?"

"They're all amazing, Alfonse," Dad complimented him. "We did have a few ideas for flavors that aren't here."

Alfonse wrinkled his nose. "In just a week's time, these are the only flavors we will have available."

"These were all great. We don't need to do my idea," I said.

"Yeah, don't worry about it," Dad agreed.

"We would like a cinnamon cake with Mexican chocolate icing as the bottom layer. Then a caramel cake with buttercream for the second. Top it with a . . ." Ms. Watson looked at Dad.

"German chocolate cake," they said at the same time.

"Okay. That was adorable," Charlie whispered to me.

Alfonse gave her a sheepish grin. "There really is no way—"

Ms. Watson cut him off. "If I can humanely fend off a boa constrictor while talking a six-year-old through landing a completely full 757 airplane, I think you can rustle up some coconut."

Alfonse paused before giving in. "Right. Why don't you two come to the counter with me and we'll get it all set up?"

"Much appreciated," Dad said gratefully.

They scooted out of their chairs and followed Alfonse.

"What was that? A boa constrictor?" I turned as I asked Charlie, but he had his phone plastered in front of his face. "Charlie?" I said after a minute.

"Oh, sorry. Just messaging Bets."

Bets.

"Wanted to capture that Ms. Watson gem before I forgot it," he said, shoving his phone back in his pocket.

"Ah," I mumbled. "Wait, I thought she didn't have a cell phone?"

"This weekend she can use the computer," he explained, not looking up from his phone. "And my messages go straight to it. She's pretty good at replying as long as she isn't playing with her brother."

Maybe now was the time to bring it all up? "Things going good with you two then?" I ventured.

"Bets is fantastic. Seriously," he insisted after seeing the look on my face. "You need to spend more time with her."

"I like her. I do! Just might take me time to get past all the old trauma."

"Well, hurry up, 'cause she's amazing."

I looked away from Charlie and his front-lit, goofy grinning mug. At the counter, Dad and Ms. Watson stood talking to Alfonse. Dad had his arm around Ms. Watson's waist. She looked at him, and they both smiled at each other. A very familiar goofy-grinning look.

The next morning things weren't any less confusing.

Bzz! Bzz!

I reached deep into the pile of leaves I had raked up and flung myself into about half an hour earlier. The desire to hoist myself out hadn't hit me. I wasn't sure it ever would.

Bzz! Bzz!

"All right, all right," I mumbled, finally finding my phone. It was a text from Charlie that read:

"Can you come over? We need to talk about something . . ."

My brain flooded with thoughts, each going in a million different directions, but one floated to the top. *He's gonna tell me they're a couple*, I thought.

Bzz! Bzz!

I chucked my phone out of the leaves but still didn't get up. Instead I fanned my arms out, then up and down through the leaves. Maybe as a Leaf Angel I could fly my way out of this. Wait. Back up, Veri. That wasn't really fair to Charlie. Feeling left out was one thing, but this other feeling I had no right to.

Bzz! Bzz!

Bzz! Bzz!

As much as I didn't want to admit it, even to myself, I was jealous, but I didn't know why. Or did I? It's probably a bad sign when you're being cryptic with yourself.

"Ugghh," I groaned as I finally stood up and faced the music. In this case "the music" was the endless *Bzz! Bzz!-*ing of my phone. In typical Charlie fashion, he had messaged me the same sentiment in a hundred different ways. I had to laugh. Was I really going to give in and lose Charlie as my best friend because of my butthead emotions? Only one way to find out.

"On my way," I texted back.

⋆ ✵ ⋆

"You all right, Veronica?" Mrs. Schwob called from the porch the third time I'd passed her house.

I had turned around a few times en route to Charlie's.

"Yeah, just avoiding imminent doom," I said cheerfully.

"That's nice!" she said absentmindedly. "Looking forward to the wedding! Gonna be a whopper!"

"Yep!"

But I could only procrastinate for so long. Eventually there was nowhere else to go.

After ringing the bell, I was expecting to see Charlie and Betsy open the door. Instead I was treated to a very odd sight in many ways.

"Veronica!" Lucia cried as she answered the door. Charlie was with her, grinning ear to ear, but the strangest thing of all was that Dr. Weathers, who I had never seen answer the door or smile, was doing both.

"Come on in," the doctor added excitedly.

"What's going on?" I asked. For some reason, I couldn't help but smile with them.

"We have some very good news," Dr. Weathers continued as they led me to the living room.

This was awkward and a little more than disheartening. How could Charlie's moms like Betsy so much that they wanted to be part of telling me that she and Charlie were a couple?

"Good news, *depending* on how you look at it," Charlie clarified, which only doubled my confusion.

"Okay . . . ," I said slowly.

All three of the Weatherses looked at each other,

waiting for one of them to speak. Until they all did at the same time.

"Veri, my dear," Lucia started.

"We've had a very important breakthrough," Dr. Weathers continued.

"They can cure you!" Charlie cut in.

Wait. What?

The words hit me like a frying pan to the face. I looked at Charlie. "Did you just say what I thought you said?"

He nodded enthusiastically. "They figured it out!"

"I-I don't . . ."

"It's true," Lucia confirmed. "Over the past few weeks we've been inching closer to isolating a cure. We believe it's something triggered in your hypothalamus."

"Or your hippocampus, but what I can say is we've officially inched over the finish line," Dr. Weathers said. "And, whatever the etiology, we can completely cure the symptoms you present with."

"Are you happy? Happy as a hippo-campus?" Charlie asked.

"My brain can't even," I managed to say.

"Understandable. It's crazy!"

"When? How?" I asked.

"First things first," Dr. Weathers instructed, "you'll need the approval of your father. Especially since he didn't sign off on our initial observations." She gave me a bit of an evil eye.

"Okay, what do I tell him you're going to do, exactly?" I asked, knowing Dad would have a lot of questions.

Dr. Weathers answered, "It's a very simple PO administration of non-synthetics."

Charlie and I looked to Lucia to translate.

"What she's saying is that it'll be a pill or something else you can easily swallow that's made of, actually, some really simple *natural* stuff, some sugar and tapioca. A mixture of organic oils. It's more about the preparation of it that will make your symptoms go away."

"Charlie . . ." My cheeks were starting to hurt from smiling.

"We'll scoot so you two can discuss."

The two women went into the kitchen, leaving me and Charlie alone on the couch. I turned to him and covered my mouth with my hands.

"I know!"

"And you're okay with this?" I asked. "You've always thought my powers were cool."

He shrugged. "I do. But I also know they can be a big pain for you."

"Thanks, Charlie."

"I'd rather have you happy than cool," he joked.

I playfully smacked his arm.

"Besides, sadly, it's not that important what I think. Are *you* okay with this?"

"Are you kidding? A life without constantly worrying that I'm going to do something mortifying at any given moment? Sign me up!" The reality of it was hitting me. Normalcy. How could anyone possibly say no to this?!

★ ✴ ★

"No. Absolutely not."

Those words didn't come out of the mouth of the person you'd expect.

I looked to Dad for backup. He was as befuddled as me.

"Why not?" he asked Ms. Watson. Then, seeing my eager expression, he added, "Not that I'm saying yes."

"Other than the basic health and safety concerns?" Ms. Watson inquired. "This 'cure' hasn't been approved by the FDA. I'd imagine it hasn't even had animal trials."

She looked at me for confirmation.

"I dunno. Probably not? Lucia said it's all natural stuff. Nothing harmful or scary. I wouldn't think you'd need FDA approval for mixing two healthy things together, right? You wouldn't be upset if I mixed brussels sprouts with lima beans."

"She's right," Dad reminded her. "And these aren't some random doctors. They've known Veri since she was tiny."

"Yeah," I agreed.

"This is too risky." Ms. Watson shook her head.

"Dad?"

He looked at me sympathetically. "I know it's exciting, but there is a lot to think about. We'll discuss and get back to you, kiddo."

I felt my jaw tighten. Here we were again. Other people making decisions about my life for me. Big decisions! And I was being cut out completely. I wanted to say something, but it wasn't a good idea. Dad was trying to be levelheaded and would totally blow a fuse if I didn't do the same. And that would completely annihilate my chances. I held my breath and nodded before going up to my room.

CHAPTER FIVE
A MOTHER OF A PROBLEM

Going back to school on a Monday is hard enough. Going back to school on a Monday when you are super-duper irritated at your father is a whole other thing.

"Veronica, do you have any more of that confetti that's shaped like wedding rings?" Dean asked me during art class.

"No," I said.

"What should we use instead?" Lizzie asked. "We don't have anything for the last few crackers."

"Leave them empty," I said in a dark tone.

They both laughed. "I'm sure there's something around

here," Lizzie said as she rummaged through the wedding craft box I had brought from home.

I continued working on the portrait but wasn't feeling it. Unfortunately, whether I was "feeling it" or not didn't matter anymore.

I had gotten a lot of nice comments from my classmates, but something about the portrait seemed off to me.

"Do you think there's something missing?" I asked Lizzie and Dean, leaning away from the canvas so they could get a look.

Lizzie tilted her head and Dean squinted his eyes at the portrait.

"It looks fantastic, art-wise. But I do think there's something that's not there," Lizzie said.

Dean nodded. "Yeah, but what?"

"I wish I knew," I sighed.

Our blank staring went on until the bell rang and I was cruelly forced to go to English class.

Please let Mr. Murray be back, I wished as I pushed the door open. Nope. Mr. Stephens was sitting at his desk, feet propped up on a set of dusty blue dictionaries. He gave me a toothy grin. I ignored it and went to my seat. Lo and behold, there was a notebook on my desk that read, in giant neon orange letters, PROPERTY OF MARK BELIEVE and, below that, MARK BELIEVE + IMAGIN-AMY = BF4EVR. Out of the corner of my eye I could see Mr. Stephens watching and pretending to hold back his laughter. He had made up a new imaginary person. Cute. The kids were eating it up. Instead of doing anything, I just walked to the back of the room where there was one empty desk next to George Antiliheese. There was always at least one empty desk next to George. I smiled at him, but there was no reaction. Phew. That meant he was already asleep. Being able to sleep with your eyes open was an impressive skill, I'd definitely give him that, but the rumor was that if you woke him up, he'd kill you. True story.

I sat down as silently as I could.

"Oh, Veronica. You spoilsport. Maybe one day you'll grow a sense of humor," Mr. Stephens said.

By the time class was over, I didn't feel at all like leaving Charlie a stupidmessage. Actually, I didn't feel like even seeing anyone the rest of the day. I was going to sneak home alone after school. First, I had to sulk through the rest of the day.

I walked down the hill toward home. About two blocks in, I noticed a familiar-looking woman leaning on a forest green SUV. Her hair was the wrong color, though.

"It couldn't be," I said to myself.

She waved when she saw me. Her other hand was occupied holding a cigarette that she quickly snuffed out when I reached her.

"Mother," I said very officially.

"Hey, Veronica," she said. "Got this." She fished the wedding invite out of her coat pocket. "I assume you sent it, not your father."

"Yeah. I, um, thought it would be nice if we could patch things up, you know?"

"Patch things up?"

I nodded.

"You still dangerous?"

"I've never been dangerous," I said softly.

She laughed. "So, the answer is 'yes,' you still have your . . . whatever."

This wasn't going at all the way I had hoped. "Yeah, but that doesn't mean I'm dangerous."

"Well, you know that means I can't be involved with you."

"That doesn't make any sense. Lots of people see me

every day and it's fine. I'm sure if you just spent some time with me—"

"Listen, it's not about that. I'm sure you are a great person, but what you have isn't natural. And that scares me. I know you are all loyal to your father for whatever reason, but since he won't get you the help you need, I can't be in your life. This is his fault. Not mine."

Oh, lady. You did not. "Dad takes care of me," I said gruffly. "He has for all these years that you've been gone." I paused to collect myself. "I just want us to be normal," I finally said.

She opened the driver's-side door and started to get in. "That would be wonderful," she said sadly. "Hit me up when you're *allowed* to be normal."

My mother slammed the door and took off, her tires squealing on the damp pavement.

I stood there trying to figure out what had just happened. In a flash my mother had reappeared and, again, ripped out any hope of making things better with her.

I needed to figure some things out.

I'd managed to get to my dad's office before Ms. Watson.

"We need to talk," I told him.

"Can you give me a minute, hun?" Dad asked through his white mask.

"Oh, uh, yeah. Hi, Bobby." In my haste I hadn't really processed that Dad still had a patient in the chair.

I went back to the waiting room and did just that until Bobby emerged and his mom took him home.

As soon as they were out the door I was back to it. Ms. Watson would be here any minute, and I needed to talk to Dad. Alone.

"I need to take the cure. You need to say yes."

"It's not that simple, Veri."

"You mean Ms. Watson doesn't approve, so you have to do what she says."

"Watch it."

I did not feel like watching it. Not one single watchy bit. I was really annoyed and didn't care if he got upset.

"It's true. If she wasn't around, you would have said it was okay yesterday. Instantly!"

"No, I wouldn't have," he said calmly.

"Liar!"

His brow furrowed and his eyes went a little dark.

"This isn't up for discussion anymore. You are out of control."

"Oh," I scoffed, "I beg to differ. I mean, I haven't blown anything up. I'm not covered in scales or set in stone." I paused for a second as I assessed my inner sitch. "Yet."

"Stop."

"That's what you want, right? You want me to be a freak for the rest of my life."

"You aren't a freak. This is just—"

"Just you making Ms. Watson happy. 'Cause that's how it is now. Just her and you. Making all the decisions. And me not mattering at all."

I was about to bust out a mother of a stupidpower, so I went outside, flinging the door open as hard as I could. The little bell that signaled when someone entered broke off and flew across the room, landing in a potted peace lily.

"Veronica," Dad warned.

Ms. Watson was pulling up just as I got outside. I opened my mouth to yell at her, but a high-pitched noise came out instead. Like a wave, it crashed over Ms. Watson's car and shattered the windshield! The shock of it was enough to jolt me out of my stupidstate, and the wave disappeared as it spread over the empty parking lot. Oh no! Had I hurt her?! I ran to her car and looked inside. She was still holding the steering wheel.

"Ms. Watson?!" I called as I tapped on the window. "I'm sorry! Are you okay?"

She opened her door and got out. "Yes, McGowan, I'm fine. Are you—"

I didn't let her finish. Now that I knew she was okay, my anger returned, surging through my system. "Good! Then I'm not sorry! I take it back." I stormed off. If they didn't want me to be normal, then I wasn't going to hold anything in anymore.

I stormed all the way to Charlie's house and up to the front door. I pushed the doorbell as hard as I could, but it wasn't very satisfying.

"Whoa, what's up?" Charlie asked when he opened the door. "You look like you might murder someone."

"Just windshields," I said as we went inside and up to his room.

We sat on the floor and I told him about what had just happened—my mom, my dad, the shattering of an innocent piece of glass.

"I don't understand why she'd be so against it," Charlie wondered.

"And why my dad won't stand up to her," I grumbled as I flopped onto my back.

Charlie let out an empathetic sigh.

"I'm sorry I . . . ," I mumbled, realizing I hadn't even bothered to check in with Charlie. "How are you?"

"Can I get you a cup of hot cocoa?"

Charlie had never offered to make me anything in the food world before. It had always been a one-way street of me providing and him eating.

"Sure," I answered.

He flew out of the room and I stayed on my back, tired from the power explosion. I thought about the look on Ms. Watson's face when I killed her windshield. Maybe my mother was right. Maybe I was dangerous. I guess if there is unintended, violent destruction of property involved, one could classify it that way. But how was I supposed to react? Dad was supposed to be on my side. But now he was on Ms. Watson's side, and I was alone. Well, almost alone.

"It's more marshmallow than cocoa!" Charlie gleefully

declared as he carried two mugs brimming with marsh-mallows into the room.

I sat up and took the hot cup. "Thanks, Charlie. This smells good!" I took a sip. "Woo! That's sweet!"

"My own special secret recipe: two packs of cocoa with half the amount of milk, and you spray whipped cream in there and stir it so it melts. Then the marshmallow extravaganza!"

"Is there sugar on the marshmallows, too?"

"Yes!" he said proudly.

"Awesome."

We quietly blew on our steaming hot cocoas for a second.

"So, you're okay?" I asked. I was thinking about what Hun Su had said in art class. "I, uh, heard something I thought maybe you might want to possibly talk about."

He had gone from happily sipping a hot cocoa to being as white as a marshmallow.

"Word in the halls is that you and Betsy are . . . a thing."

"We aren't a couple," he said quietly, still holding the cocoa near his mouth.

"Excuse me?" I had never heard Charlie choose to speak so softly.

"Veri...," he groaned, which irritated the heck out of me.

"Why did I have to hear this from Hun Su?" I did my best not to sound jealous.

"Because there's nothing to hear!" He took a big gulp of cocoa, then gasped. "Hot! Very ridiculously hot!"

"You like her?" I asked.

He shrugged.

"You're killing me."

"Yeah, I do. I think I do," he finally admitted. His marshmallow-white face was now looking more cherry red.

"Okay," I said slowly, trying to think it through. "And she likes you?"

"I dunno."

"You haven't said anything to her about it?"

"Why would I do that?!"

"Because apparently everyone in school—except for me, your blooming best friend—knows about it. You kinda have to." I took a deep breath. Why was everything turning into a fight today?

We sipped in silence for a few more minutes.

"Will you help me?"

"Help you what?"

"Tell Betsy."

"I think that's kinda between you two."

"I don't mean that you'd tell her. You'll just help me find a way to tell her. I have no clue how to tell a girl that."

"Neither do I."

"Please, Veri," he asked genuinely.

I looked at him for a minute. How could I say no? He was my best friend. And he looked so very, very pathetic.

"Okay," I agreed.

"Thank you." He sighed with relief. "Always feels better to come clean with you."

I'd sealed my fate. Charlie would be off with Betsy and Dad and Ms. Watson in wedded bliss; I'd be alone.

But I didn't have to be.

"Charlie, I need to talk to your moms."

* ✳ ✦

I sat on the exam table and waited. Charlie had wedged himself on one of the counters below a cabinet.

"Am I doing the right thing?" I whispered to Charlie.

He nodded. "If it's what you want, then yes."

I couldn't even conceive of a day without powers, but it was about to happen. I could live like a normal kid! The nervous butterflies in my stomach were getting more excited.

"Everyone ready?" Lucia asked when she and Dr. Weathers came back into the room.

"Yep," I said.

"And Rik knows about this?" Dr. Weathers asked.

"We talked about the cure extensively just this morning," I said as confidently as I could.

"Well, then. Here we go," Lucia said with a smile.

With latex-laden hands, Dr. Weathers opened up a small aluminum canister. Bright white vapor poured out of it.

"Dramatic," Charlie commented.

Once the fog had drifted away, she removed something with a long pair of tweezers.

"Take this and you should see a marked improvement within the next twenty-four hours," Dr. Weathers said, offering me what was clenched betwixt the tweezers.

"Um, is this a joke?" I asked, and looked around. I was expecting a camera crew to burst through the door.

Dr. Weathers raised an eyebrow.

I pointed at the fancy-schmancy, scientific-breakthrough cure. "Hate to break it to ya, but that's a gummy bear."

Dr. Weathers gave Lucia an "I told you so" look.

"We had the molds and I thought it was cute," Lucia said. "Plus, if Veri was nervous, I thought it might be easier to eat a cure shaped like a friendly gummy bear." She shrugged and gave me a wink.

"I can guarantee you this is not a joke," Dr. Weathers assured me.

"So, I just eat this gummy bear, and my powers are gone? Forever?" I asked.

"We'll still be doing research on your condition, as this is just for your symptoms and not what causes them," Dr. Weathers explained.

"Well, all right then. Down the hatch!" I said much more loudly than I intended. Those excited butterflies in my stomach were now biting their fingernails. Charlie and I looked nervously at each other.

I grabbed the gummy bear from the tweezers and flung it into my mouth. I chewed and swallowed before I could think about it anymore. Once it had settled, I had only one comment: "Strawberry-y."

"Ooh, can I have one?" Charlie asked.

Both Dr. Weathers and Lucia stared at me silently.

"I don't need to stay here for the next twenty-four hours, do I?"

Lucia laughed. "No, no. Sorry."

"But let us know if you have any undesirable side effects," Dr. Weathers added.

"Like what?" I asked nervously. "I didn't know that was a thing."

"Don't worry about it! You'll be fine!" Lucia told me.

"You feel fine, right?" Dr. Weathers asked.

I nodded.

"Excellent."

"Shouldn't we, like, test her or something?" Charlie asked his moms. "Do something that would make her superpowers work and see what happens?"

"Not yet, Charlie," she said. "We need to give the cure time to do its thing."

Both doctors stared at me expectantly.

"So, uh, is there something else?" I couldn't help but ask.

"No! We're just excited," Lucia explained. "We'll be patient from now on. I promise."

"Okay . . . thanks for fixing me!"

"Wanna stay for dinner?" Charlie asked.

"Actually, what would you two say to us dropping you at the mall for pizza? We should log a few things," Dr. Weathers said, already looking at her tablet.

"Sure!" I definitely didn't want to go home yet.

"Great. One of us will pick you up later and drop you home."

"And maybe we can figure out that thing we were talking about upstairs," Charlie whispered.

"Maybe," I whispered back.

At the mall, I decided to do something. Again, I'd need some specialized help, so I went to see Ted and ask him to get another message to my mom.

"She is not the nicest human mammal," Ted said, shaking his head at the note I was trying to give him.

"She's just misunderstood."

"She threw a shoe at me."

"Just, you know, slip it under her door or something. You don't need to physically hand it over. Please?" I asked nicely.

He took the note from me. "If I die by stiletto . . ."

"I will avenge thee," I joked.

He took the note from me.

"Thank you."

"Where's Charlie?"

"Getting our pizza."

Ted shook his head and pointed. "Sorry, I meant *there's* Charlie."

Charlie handed me my slice when he joined us. "So, did you ask Ted what I should do?"

Boy, he was jumping right into it, wasn't he?

"You mean about Betsy?" I asked.

"Yeah!"

"Betsy?" Ted asked, "Like, *grr* Betsy?"

"Yeah. She's going to be my girlfriend," Charlie said cheerfully.

"Nice."

"He hasn't said anything to her," I explained.

"Little dude, the time is now!" Ted declared.

The wheels in my brain began to turn. The sooner he told her, the sooner I'd lose him.

"But we really need to figure out the right way to tell her, remember?" I said.

"Aw, man, listen to your heart," Ted recommended. "Take it from a big dude who has been there."

Charlie looked at me. "He's got a point. How many girls have you professed your love to?"

"B-but, I can give insight. I *am* a girl!"

"Next time you see her, bro, just tell her what's in your heart." Ted nodded.

I did not like this.

"I hate to say it, Veri, but I kind of like this plan," Charlie said.

"It's not a plan!" I scoffed. "We need to take some serious time and figure this out. Like a week or two. Maybe a month tops!"

Both Ted and Charlie shook their heads.

"No. I will drown in my emotions by then," Charlie said. "I'm going to tell her tomorrow."

"Right on, little man!" Ted high-fived Charlie and told me, "Let love blossom naturally, girly."

So it was decided. And I couldn't say a single thing about it.

Lucia drove me home a little bit later. Dad was working at his night job as a bouncer at a local club, so at least I wouldn't have to see him until the morning. I hadn't felt any difference and now I was wondering if I was really supposed to. It wasn't every day your superpowers were taken from you. In superhero movies, this would cause the titular character to fall to their knees and cry out to the sky about their cool thing being taken away. But getting rid of my powers was the highlight of my year. Sure, I'd had the crappiest day and tomorrow was shaping up to be a best friend–losing doozy, but at least it felt like a fresh start. I hadn't had even the smallest stupidpowers outburst all day! A normal life. I fell asleep with a gigantic grin on my face.

CHAPTER SIX
TRANSFORMATION TUESDAY

"Good morning!" I called as I flew down the stairs.

As I had expected, Dad was sitting at the breakfast table, ready to sentence me. But I was prepared. "Listen, I know you are probably mucho mad at me about the windshield and I'm prepared to work in the office to pay Ms. Watson back for fixing it."

Dad crossed his arms. "A: I'm not mad at you for busting the windshield. I'm concerned by your attitude that *led* to the busting of the windshield. B: What the heck got into you today? You are not the girl from yesterday."

"I'm not!" I said. And I really felt it. The sheer excitement of a day without stupidpowers was making me giddy. "That windshield-smashing girl is gone, Dad, I promise."

"That's a pretty big promise."

"I can do it," I said confidently as I got my things together for school.

"We can talk about the windshield later. Just please apologize to her today, okay? Properly?"

"Can do!"

"I don't know what's up, but I'm digging this attitude," he told me.

It was a huge change, for sure. True, he didn't know why things had changed. I still hadn't even thought how I was going to tell him about that. Later. After the wedding. From the plan I had brewing, it might not even matter after that.

Charlie wasn't at our meeting spot, so I started walking without him. It wasn't until I was a block from school that he caught up with me.

"Are you secretly on some Olympic-level speed-walking

team or something?" Charlie gasped. You could see his breath in the cool morning air.

"Where were you? Sleep in?" I asked. Then I had a much scarier thought. "Did you tell her?!"

"No, I haven't yet. I want to do it face-to-face. When the time is right, you know?" he said excitedly.

Once we got to our lockers, something hit me. "Oh! Crud! No more stupidmessaging!" I said. "What do we do now?"

"Yeah . . ." Charlie scratched his head.

"Guess we could do paper notes?" I suggested.

"What is this, 1982?!" he scoffed.

"Could be fun. Leave them in each other's lockers. Slip them to each other in the hall. Like spies."

"Ohhh. Let's do it!" he agreed.

(I knew that spy bit would work.)

"I'll let you know when I do the thing," he told me with a wink as he dumped his bag and coat in the bottom of his locker.

I hung up my backpack and took off my coat. "You know, you don't have to rush it."

"Love is a fickle beast, Veri. You gotta act on it before

it's gone," he said dramatically as he slammed his locker and playfully sauntered down the hall.

My heart sank. *Did he just say "love"?*

I tried to shake it off, but the sound of Charlie using the *L*-word to describe his feelings for Betsy put me in a trance for all of homeroom. I couldn't even pay attention when the Tech Twins were doing the announcements. All I really gleaned was that the lunch special was meatloaf.

After that I wandered to the art room, where I knew I could at least drown in the art and not think about things for a little bit.

"Good job on the announcements," I told Lizzie and Dean. "Looking forward to that meatloaf."

"Never eat the meatloaf," Dean said.

I chuckled.

"No, seriously, don't," Lizzie said with a straight face.

I went back to sketching and felt it start to lighten my mood. It was so nice to feel my emotions without fearing them!

"That is some spectacular work, Veronica," Mrs. Brannon said as I started packing up before the bell.

"Thanks. I was really in the zone today."

"It shows!" she said, and gave me a pat on the shoulder.

Then the dread hit me. English class. UGH. But wait! I didn't have to worry about my stupidpowers flaring up! I could say and do whatever I wanted. I could get even.

"Mrs. Brannon? Can I be excused a few minutes early?" I asked.

"Sure," she said, waving me off.

I grabbed my stuff, ran to my locker, and scooped up every notebook I had. There weren't enough, so I opened Charlie's locker and dug through the wasteland at the bottom. "How is it so messy in here already?!" There I found many abandoned notebooks that didn't have any writing on them or in them. Perfect. I wrote as I ran, flipping over the notebooks as I scribbled on the covers. It wasn't my most pristine work, but it was very effective.

The bell rang, and I was ready and waiting. As the class before ours trailed out of Mr. Murray's English room, I kept an eye out for Mr. Stephens. As the last student left, so did he.

Yes, I said to myself.

I ran into the classroom and quickly set a notebook on each desk, saving a very special one for Mr. Stephens's desk. I was tired of him thinking he was so cool for picking on me. And, honestly, tired of the other kids thinking he was cool, too. They needed to see what Mr. Stephens really was: a control freak and a bully. I knew that if the joke was at his expense, he would lose his cool. And that's exactly what I wanted—even if it landed me in the principal's office.

Then I went across the hall and waited, watching my classmates enter. One by one they went in, and a few seconds later I'd hear them laugh. Excellent. I wished Charlie could be there to see it.

Finally, Mr. Stephens returned and I followed him in. All the kids were standing around the edges of classroom giggling.

"Well, hello," he said to them. "What's going on here?"

I slid in unnoticed with the other kids as Mr. Stephens approached his desk. He spotted the notebook I'd left him. "Oh, hardy-har-har," he said, then looked for me. I ducked behind one of the basketball players. "Has she left one on all of your desks, too?" he asked, then walked around the room checking. "She did. An entire classroom of imaginary students, including an imaginary teacher!"

The kids giggled. I stood on my tiptoes to get a view. Mr. Stephens was obviously embarrassed by the kids laughing. Suddenly he let out a giant laugh. "Ha! Well, it looks like Imagin-Amy is going to be the teacher today, or at least that's what it says on my desk."

Oh, crud. He was trying to go with it so the kids didn't laugh at him.

"Maybe she will take on one human student?" he asked my classmates as he flicked one of my notebooks off the desk in the center of the room. "Yep. Looks like Ian-maginary will give up his seat!"

The kids started to laugh *with* him. My plan was backfiring!

"What are we going to learn today, teacher?" he asked Imagin-Amy. "It's a shame that there isn't space for the other students today. I think *someone* thought they could get me to lose my temper and show that I can't take a joke." He surveyed his audience, my classmates. "I'll just have to be a big old meanie. Or . . ." A sly grin spread across his face. ". . . Give all of you the day off!" Mr. Stephens laughed loudly as he put his feet up on the desk. "No teacher, no seats, no class! What else can I do? I'll just be here wasting taxpayer money!"

The class went berserk! Everyone was cheering, and Mr. Stephens was basking in the love. Gross.

"Mr. Stephens!" a very irritated southern drawl bellowed from the open doorway.

Mr. Stephens nearly fell out of his chair! I pushed to the front of the group of students to see what was happening.

"What in heaven's name are you doing to my students?!" Mr. Murray asked him.

Mr. Stephens stood up, shocked. He quickly scanned the room until he found me and pointed. "I-it was Veronica McGowan!"

Mr. Murray shook his head in confusion and turned to me. "Miss Veronica, could you enlighten an old man about this frivolity happening in his very own learning sanctuary?"

I loved Mr. Murray.

"Well, sir. I'm not sure why Mr. Stephens is singling me out presently, but these are the facts: Mr. Stephens invented an imaginary friend on our first day of school," I began.

Mr. Murray raised his eyebrows, and Mr. Stephens started to visibly sweat.

"Well, that's not entirely—" Mr. Stephens started.

"Don't interrupt," Mr. Murray scolded him.

I continued, "And every day he made that imaginary

friend more and more part of our class. He even gave her a name."

"It's not—" He tried to interrupt again.

"Imagin-Amy," one of my classmates chimed in.

"Oh, all of you were in on it," Mr. Stephens said under his breath.

There were a few gasps as the other kids began to turn on Mr. Stephens.

"He was bullying Veronica, Mr. Murray!" Evelyn Baker called from the back of the room.

"Yeah!" a few other students agreed.

"Bullying? Please, Evelyn," Mr. Stephens scoffed. "The only one here who has been bullied is me. And it was by you when you sang Ave Maria at the talent show."

"Mr. Stephens, did you just chastise a child?" Mr. Murray was horrified.

"I think I'm done here," Mr. Stephens said with a big, fake smile, ignoring what Mr. Murray had said.

There was a lot of muffled laughter as Mr. Stephens grabbed his things.

"Settle down, class, and kindly take your seats," Mr. Murray instructed.

I made sure to linger long enough that Mr. Stephens and I would cross paths as he left.

"You'd think after all these years a sense of humor would have grown on you!" I said quietly as he stomped by.

He narrowed his eyes and shook his head at me.

I pretty much floated through the rest of the day. If I had my powers, I probably really would have! But also, if I had my powers, I never would have stood up to Mr. Stephens for fear that they would flare up. So, there ya go. I took a very detailed account of what had happened in a note for Charlie. When I popped it in his locker, I couldn't help but worry what was waiting for me in mine. There was a green, ragged piece of paper folded into an uneven square waiting on top of my math workbook. I took it but hesitated before opening it. Everything was really about to change. Charlie would have a girlfriend. And here I had thought it was weird to say my dad had a girlfriend. Saying Charlie did was one hundred times weirder. Thinking it was Betsy was about a million times weirder still.

I exhaled sharply and opened the note before I could think anymore. Charlie had written extensively about his breakfast and what he planned on having for lunch, then at the bottom he had added, "Haven't told her yet! Gonna make it special and tell her after school today, so don't wait for little romantic me!"

I didn't. As soon as the last bell rang, I began a victory march home.

Now *that* was a day at school. I had forgotten just how much easier things were without powers. I could go back to focusing on Normal Kid stuff! I bounded down the hill. At the intersection I was thrilled to see a familiar green SUV.

CHAPTER SEVEN
A MOTHER OF A PROBLEM, THE SEQUEL

I looked around to make sure there weren't any witnesses. I would tell Dad and Charlie about this . . . when the time was right. Given how no one was trusting me to make decisions lately, I wasn't going to waste an opportunity by handing over my decision-making power this time.

"Hi," I said quietly as I got in the passenger seat and put my seatbelt on.

"My place okay?" my mother asked.

"Sure." Getting asked to my mother's house the first time we were hanging out was funny. Not ha-ha funny, but amusing considering I had yet to be invited to Ms.

Watson's house. We drove a few minutes to the east side of town and parked in front of a brown brick duplex.

"I didn't know you lived so close."

"It's a fairly new development. Come on in."

She led me up the short set of stairs and unlocked the door. Once I stepped inside, I noticed a definite decorating style.

"You like figurines?" I asked.

A broad smile covered her face. "Yes, I'm a bit of an addict," she confessed.

Addicted would be a descriptive, apt word for sure. All the shelves, every ledge, and even the top of the refrigerator were covered in small ceramic statues. Most of them were of cute children doing old-timey things like carrying buckets or talking on a rotary phone.

"How about a glass of milk?" she asked.

"I'm okay," I answered.

She went into the kitchen, which was just on the other side of a breakfast counter. She poured a glass of milk anyway and brought it to me.

"Cheers," she said, and sat down on the couch. I followed.

Then it was quiet. I certainly didn't know what to say.

"I like that one," I said, pointing to a figurine of an elf that was holding a microphone.

"Oh, that's Elvis," she said with a small laugh. "He and Ignacio are never apart."

I looked next to Elvis and saw what must have been Ignacio: a statue of a turtle with a dripping bucket of paint resting on the back of its shell.

"Cute," I said.

Then it went silent again. I took a few long sips of milk. It wasn't very cold.

"So, the last time I saw you, things went badly," she said hesitantly. "And I guess the time before that went really badly."

That was true. If you wanted me to be all police-reporty about it, I would describe what would be considered an attempted kidnapping, followed by Agent/Ms. Watson stepping in and keeping the mother away. Then, unfortunately, the spited mother called the troubled daughter all sorts of not-friendly names and may have implied that she was a freak of nature.

"It wasn't that bad," I offered.

"Sometimes things get out of hand," she said. "Just

happens. I hope you know I only wanted what was best for you."

I nodded. "I'm sorry."

She let out a sigh. "You shouldn't need to be sorry, Veronica. What has happened to you—you can't control that. Or couldn't? But now?"

"Uh, yeah! I'm cured. Charlie's moms are scientists and they found a way!"

"You're cured now?"

"Yep!"

She looked at me, unsure.

"You can scare me or, you know, make me mad or whatever. It won't make my powers flare up."

"Powers? That's how they work?"

I hadn't even realized. She was so not part of my life that she didn't even know we called them powers or how they were triggered.

"That was our, uh, best guess. Emotional stress. Different things happen. *Would* happen. Still trying to get used to that."

"Right on," she said.

"I mean, something definitely would have happened

today. Mr. Stephens had been kind of a jerk to me at school."

"Jason Stephens?" she said bitterly. "Yuck."

I giggled. "Yeah, that's how I feel about him, too. He's not my favorite teacher by any means."

"And Agent—I mean, *Ms. Watson* is a teacher there now, too?" she asked.

"No, she's a guidance counselor."

"So weird."

"She's actually pretty good at it," I said. Why did I say that? Something made me instantly defend Ms. Watson. My mother didn't seem to notice.

"And now your father is getting married to that woman?" she continued. "Blows my mind."

"Mine, too," I confessed.

"Really?"

I nodded again. It felt weird to be so honest with her. Actually, it felt kind of good.

"Is she good at taking care of you?"

"Ms. Watson is . . . different," I said.

"Suppose you'll be calling her Mom soon enough, huh?" she asked. She got a cigarette out of her purse and put it in her mouth. She was about to light it, but then stopped after she spotted me. It was almost like she had forgotten I was there for a second. "Sorry." She tucked the cigarette behind her ear.

"I don't think I'll ever call her Mom. She doesn't really do traditional 'mom-type' things."

"Good. I'm your only mom ever," she said fiercely, then gave a sharp laugh. "I wish I had more of a say in that. Being your mom, I mean."

"You do," I assured her.

She nodded. "There's been a lot I've wanted to say to you. Like, it's okay to be freaked out by your powers. You know that, right? Rik wants you to think they're great and all, but it's okay to disagree. That's why I'm here now. To be a good influence. So you have someone on your side, you know?"

I took a sip of my milk and then put it on the end table, sliding it between two matching baby figurines.

"How is everything else? School? That friend of yours . . . the boy with the accent . . ."

"Charlie," I refreshed her memory.

"You two a couple yet?"

I laughed. "No! No. He's my best friend." I paused. "Or, he was my best friend. I'm not sure anymore."

"You get in a fight or something?"

"No. He's just been busy with . . ." I trailed off, not knowing how to phrase it.

"Ah! Another woman," she declared.

"He's been hanging out with his friend—our friend—Betsy a lot."

"That's how it goes. Men find new friends and other lovers. Suddenly you're obsolete."

I thought about Dad and Ms. Watson.

"And it can't be easy being the third wheel with your father and that woman."

She had read my mind. "I don't think they think that."

"They will. How could they not?" She shrugged. "But anyway, let's do something fun, shall we? Do you like board games?" She dug under the coffee table and produced a deck of UNO cards.

"Sure," I agreed.

We played a few rounds before my phone began to buzz.

"Aren't you a little young to have one of those?" my mother asked.

"Dad says it's for safety." I added, "He doesn't know I'm here."

"Maybe let's keep it that way," my mother said, rolling her eyes playfully.

I giggled and then looked at my phone. It was Dad just warning me that he ordered the asparagus side dish with our dinner, and that I was going to try it. I hated asparagus. "I should get going," I told her, having also noticed the time.

"No problem."

"Can I use your bathroom before we go?"

She nodded. "Down the hall to the left."

Walking down the hall I noticed that there were two bedrooms. One was obviously her bedroom, but the other was filled with boxes and Christmas decorations. A room waiting for someone to fill it.

She drove me to a few blocks from our house, so that we wouldn't be spotted.

"Wanna hang out again tomorrow? I think you owe me a rematch," she asked.

"Yeah, I'd like that . . . Mom."

"Great! Same time, same place, doodlebug!"

I waved to her as she drove away, then headed home—though I was starting to wonder how much longer it would be my home.

"Help yourself." Dad pointed to the stack of Thai food takeout containers in the kitchen.

"What are you guys doing?" I asked, looking into the living room. It was an odd sight; they were both holding their left hands in the air and looking at them.

"Rings came," Ms. Watson told me.

"Oh, neat. Can I see?" I asked as I rushed up to them.

They both pulled the shiny gold bands off and plopped them into my hand. "You two are so traditional," I commented as I twirled the bands around in the light. I noticed some writing inside each of them. Squinting, I read "Two hearts . . ." engraved in one band and "beat as one" in the other.

"Can't go wrong with U2," my dad said confidently.

"Yeah," I said weakly. I handed them the rings. "Mind if I eat in my room? I have some major homework."

"Sure. Get to it, go-getter," Dad said.

"Do you need assistance?" Ms. Watson asked as I left the room. It was the first time she'd offered to help with homework, so both Dad and I turned to look at her strangely. "Do you?" she repeated.

"Uh, nope," I said. "Thanks, though." Oh, no . . . I forgot that I was supposed to . . . "Ms. Watson. I, um, really want to apologize for my behavior, um, when I murdered your windshield. Please let me know how much it cost to fix and I will repay you."

Dad nodded at me.

"I'm really, *really* sorry."

He gave me a thumbs-up.

"I accept your apology, McGowan. It takes a great deal of maturity to admit when you've acted inappropriately, especially when you are in the pre-adulthood, post-child stage of your life. So, well done. And no need to repay me. Insurance covered it."

". . . Thanks," I said slowly. "I'll be upstairs if you need me." As I left I spotted my dad giving Ms. Watson the same thumbs-up he gave me.

Upstairs, I messaged Charlie. A few seconds later, the video messaging app on my computer trilled.

"Hey!" I said nervously. "I thought you'd be out on a date."

"Timing wasn't right," Charlie sighed, and conked his head on the camera. "I'll tell her tomorrow."

"Maybe it's a sign that the timing will never be right?" I ventured.

"It'll be right tomorrow," he said confidently.

"How do you know that?"

"I just do."

I laughed.

"What?" he asked.

"Nothing," I said. "You might want to wipe off your camera. You got it a little greasy."

He wiped it with his shirttail while talking. "Seriously, why the laughs?"

"It wasn't a laugh-laugh. It was just a life-is-weird laugh," I explained.

"That really is of no help, V."

I paused and gathered my thoughts. I wanted to say this in the smartest way possible. "What do you like about Betsy? I mean, it's Betsy." Oh, Veronica.

"I dunno. I mean, she's—"

"A riot?" I teased him.

"Yes! And she's who she is, you know."

"Yeah."

It was quiet for a second.

"How did you know that you liked her?" I asked.

He chewed on his lip for a minute before saying, "I guess I just did."

"Hmm."

"Feels kinda odd talking about it," he said quietly.

"Sorry," I said quickly. "You were just so eager to talk about it and . . . love earlier."

"True," he said, then laughed. "I don't know. Just feels weird right now."

"Okay . . ." We stared at each other on the screen until we cracked up. "You know what's really weird?"

"Please tell me. I can't stand any type of suspense," Charlie said.

"Dad had lyrics from a U2 song engraved on their wedding bands."

"That man and his eighties tunes. Gotta love it."

And we talked on and on like that until he fell asleep in front of the computer. I couldn't help but stay awake. As far as I was concerned, it was the last night when Charlie was mine.

Now, I don't want to freak anyone out, but the next day at
school I had a pretty big surprise. And that surprise was a
big old nothing. Nothing. Absolutely nothing strange or
embarrassing or emoji-creating happened! I went to class,
I did my art, I blessed the stars in the sky for Mr. Murray's
health, and I waited for a note from Charlie to arrive in my
locker. When it did, it was brief. Well, after the daily food
rundown, of course. He hadn't told her yet. It made me
wish I hadn't made plans to hang out with my mom. Then
at least I could have had a little more Charlie time. Part of
me had felt guilty for not telling him last night that I had
been with her and was planning on meeting up again. I
guess the other part of me knew that I needed to make
sure things were good before telling anyone. This had to
be perfect. My future was kind of riding on it.

"There you go," my mom said as she handed me the glass
of milk, just like the day before.

"Thanks," I said.

"Wanna play some cards, then watch a little TV before
you go?"

"Yeah, that sounds great," I told her.

"I always watch *Wheel of Fortune*. Every day," she said. "Never missed one."

"Really? What about yesterday?"

"Oh, I looked before I got you—it was a rerun."

"Phew!" I feigned relief.

She got out the UNO deck and we played until *Wheel of Fortune* came on. Once it was done she reached for her pack of cigarettes.

"Oops," she said, realizing what she was doing. "I'm a creature of routine. Guess I need to change it up if you're going to be around more often."

"Guess so," I said. "Hope it's not a big deal!"

"Me, too," she said, her fingers twitching with the unlit cigarette between them.

CHAPTER EIGHT
NOTABLE NOTES

The next day I was almost mauled on the way to school by a beast called Charlie.

"I told her!" he squeaked, then coughed and forced his voice down an octave. "I told her."

"Holy moly," I said. My first instinct was to feel around for a stupidpower, but then I remembered I didn't need to. "So you are . . . coupled?"

"Well," he began, "I may have told her very late last night. Over messenger. And I fell asleep."

"How could you fall asleep?!"

"Stress coma!" he said, like that was the natural thing to do.

"What do you have to be stressed about?"

"She could say that I'm just too darn handsome to date. Or, you know, that she thinks I'm awful," he said, a trace of self-doubt twinging his voice.

"Oh, hush. You're wonderful," I said, then felt heat rise to my cheeks. "Anyway, remember me when you're off in Coupleville with all the other couples playing couples tennis or whatever you do."

"What are you talking about? Nothing's going to change," he said, shocked.

"You've seen Dad and Ms. Watson, right?" I said. I could feel myself getting upset, but even though I knew I wasn't going to have a power surge, I wanted to get out of there. "I'm going to swing past the art room before homeroom, okay?" I said and went in the opposite direction before he could answer. "Let me know when to say proper congratulations!" I called over my shoulder. Then I wiped a stupid tear off of my stupid cheek.

After every class that day I checked my locker, waiting for The Note from Charlie, but class after class it didn't show.

At the end of the day it finally appeared. I unfolded it quickly. "Haven't seen her yet—finally got put in boys' health class. Boo. Boys are gross," it said. I wrote Charlie a quick note telling him to text me when he could and that I had to do stuff after school. "Stuff" equaled seeing my mom again. I went over to his locker and unlocked it. Might as well get a piece of gum while I was there. As usual, a few things spilled out onto the floor, so I leaned over, set both notes on the ground, and tried to sweep the other debris back into its home. Within our mess, I noticed our notes from the day before.

"Well, well, Veronica McGowan. Looks like someone has been passing notes in school."

For farts' sake.

Above me stood Mr. Stephens, happy as a clam. (I'll never understand that saying. Are clams naturally happy? Do people think their shells are smiling? If anything, I'd say they look indecisive. "Indecisive as a clam" should be the saying.)

"Let's go!" he sang as he snatched the notes up from the pile of rubble that had escaped Charlie's locker.

"Those are just pieces of paper," I said as I closed the locker.

"These are notes."

"If they *are* notes, who cares? It's not like I was passing them during class."

"Possession is nine-tenths of the law," he said proudly. "Principal's office. Now."

He walked behind me the whole way and told the receptionist of my horrible crimes. He then turned over the notes, including the old ones and one on purple paper, which I hadn't seen.

Mr. Stephens scanned the open notes. "Looks like you need to call in Betsy Monroe and Charles Weathers, too. They seem to be her accomplices."

"We'll let their—" the receptionist started, but Mr. Stephens interrupted.

"Don't worry, I'll do it." He barged behind the desk and went to the corner where the morning announcement station was set up. He flicked on the power switch and talked into the receiver. "Betsy Monroe and Charles Weathers, please report to the principal's office. Now." His eyes twinkled as he looked at me.

"We'll take it from here, Mr. Stephens," the annoyed receptionist told him.

"How's that sense of humor holding up?" he asked me as he walked out the door.

The receptionist took the handful of notes into the back offices. A few minutes later, Charlie and Betsy arrived within seconds of each other.

"What's going on?" Charlie asked.

"Stephens found our notes," I grumbled. "Decided to make a federal case out of it."

"He's the worst," Charlie groaned.

"Are you okay, Betsy?" I asked. She was white as a ghost.

"I'm fine," she said, but she didn't look at either of us.

"It's okay, we won't get in that much trouble," Charlie reassured her. Then he leaned over and whispered to me, "I hope."

"Vice Principal Andrews will see you now," the receptionist said when he returned.

"Vice Principal?!" Charlie whispered again to me. "We are in big trouble if we have to talk to her!"

"Sit, kids," Miss Andrews said with a small smile. She was the nicest of the office staff, for sure, but it seemed like overkill for such a small offense.

"Normally the guidance counselor would handle this, but since Ms. Watson is set to be your stepmother soon, Veronica, it poses a conflict of interest and I had to step in."

I looked at the clock on the wall to my right. I needed to motor. I was already late to meet Mom.

"Late for something?" Miss Andrews asked.

"Uh, no," I said meekly.

"Well, being as I don't really care about this note stuff,

you all can go. And here. Finish it up *outside* of school, please?" She handed us each a few of the confiscated notes. We all shoved them into our bags and pockets as quickly as possible.

The three of us looked at each other excitedly. We hustled towards the door before she could change her mind.

"No more notes in class," she warned.

"Aye-aye, Captain!" Charlie saluted her.

"Thank you!" I said.

Betsy gave her a meaningful head nod.

"Oh, see you on Saturday," Vice Principal Andrews said after us. "Event of the season!"

* ✳ *

Seconds later we burst out the front entrance like we had escaped hard prison time. Everyone else had gone home, and the front of the school was completely abandoned.

"I can't even believe that!" Charlie said, bewildered.

"I know!" I agreed.

"VP definitely became slightly cool," Betsy observed.

My revelry stopped immediately. In the drop-off circle

in front of the school there was an SUV with a black-haired woman leaning against it and smoking a cigarette.

"Crud."

"Veri?" Charlie asked as my mom waved to me.

"I was worried about you!" she called out between drags on her cigarette. "You weren't at our meeting spot at the meeting time!"

"Is that . . ." Charlie squinted, obviously trying to figure out if it was my mom.

"It's her," I confirmed.

Betsy stepped in front of me. "What do you want?" she called out.

Mom cackled. "Who's this? I like her."

"It's okay," I told them, and moved out from behind Betsy.

"No! It's definitely not!" Charlie protested.

"I saw her the past few days. We hung out. It's fine. She's fine."

"Veri!"

"We're trying to fix things. Okay? I'm going to go with her."

"Not alone you aren't," Betsy snorted.

"Seriously, it's fine. I've been alone with her a couple times already." I started walking toward my mom, but Betsy and Charlie followed me all the way to the car.

"Hi, Charlie," Mom said.

"Hi?" Charlie said suspiciously.

"I'm Veronica's mom." She offered her hand to Betsy, who barely grabbed her fingertips.

"Betsy."

"Ready to go?" Mom asked me.

"Yes," Betsy and Charlie said in unison.

"Bye, friends, see you later," I told them through gritted teeth. They did not need to come with us.

"Yep, we'll see you in the car, and then wherever you are going, and then safely back home," Betsy answered.

"Well then," Mom said, giving me the eye, "let's go."

"Aren't we going to your place?" I asked as we drove in the opposite direction.

"I'm thinking we might go somewhere with a little more space since there are so many of us. If we are going to wreck our schedule, we might as well enjoy it," Mom said, turning on the blinker to head over the bridge leading past the oil refinery and toward the national forest.

"If she whacks us in the woods, I'm gonna be so mad," Betsy whispered to me.

Much to my surprise (and secret relief), Mom quickly flipped on her turn signal again and pulled into the gravel parking lot of Dairy Dee-light, the ice cream shop.

"I had a major ice cream craving," she told us. "Let's get our sugar on!"

"This is bribery," Charlie told me as we waited in line. "Very good, effective bribery, but bribery nonetheless."

As we got out of the car, I nudged Charlie. "So?" I asked quietly.

"We haven't gotten a chance to talk yet," he whispered back as we got in line.

"But you have literally all your classes together." I didn't understand.

"She was in the art room for a project almost all day. Didn't you see her?"

"What does everyone want?" Mom asked as we moved quickly to the window.

"Uh, get me whatever. I'm going to the bathroom," Betsy said, and buzzed around the corner.

"When nature calls," Mom mused.

Once we had our sweet treats, we sat at one of the picnic tables next to the river.

I took a bite of my cherry-dipped cone and waited for someone else to start the conversation.

"So why now?" Charlie filled the void.

"'Why now' what?" Mom asked after a sip of milkshake.

Charlie dug through his sundae, separating the gumballs from the ice cream. "This sundae always seems brilliant until I go to eat it . . . ," he mumbled to himself.

"I think Charlie wants to know why you are here now. And wanting to talk to Veronica," Betsy answered for him. She had come back from the bathroom and sat next to me. She was really going overboard with the protective thing.

"Because she's my daughter," Mom said defensively. "Besides, I don't need to answer to any of you. It's Veronica's and my relationship. Not yours." Mom's own words made her realize something and her eyes went wide. "Oh, the other woman . . ."

I choked on a bit of ice cream coating.

"*Umm!*" I almost shouted, "Betsy is going to be the videographer at the wedding, aren't you, Betsy?" It was

146

the first thing I thought of. Not great, but it changed the course of the conversation.

"Yep," she said. "You aren't coming, are you?"

"That would be a really bad scene," Charlie agreed.

"These two are your little bulldogs, aren't they?" Mom said to me. "Don't worry. I wasn't planning on crashing the party," she told them, but then gave me a little wink.

"Well, that was bizarro," Charlie said as we watched the SUV zip away from us.

"She's not that bad, right?" I asked.

"She doesn't seem that great either," Betsy said.

"Other than the free ice cream."

"I better go. I think the blue line leaves soon," Betsy told us.

"You want me to walk you?" Charlie asked.

"That's very thoughtful, Charlie, but . . . I'm kinda worried Veronica's mom is gonna come back or something. Maybe you should go with her."

"She won't," I said. "You don't need to worry about me."

"Besides, it's out of the way," Betsy said. "Really, thank you, though. I'll, uh, see you tomorrow."

Before we could say anything else, she sprinted out of sight.

"So you two never talked about it?" I asked Charlie while we walked home.

"When could we?"

"True."

"And it would be awkward to talk about it in front of you," Charlie said, then quickly added, "in front of anyone. Actually."

"Yeah. Oh, gosh, yeah."

We said our good nights and I went home. That was a very normal day. Getting in trouble for normal things. Why did it feel kind of blah?

After I got ready for bed, I pulled out of my pocket the small pile of notes that Vice Principal Andrews had given back to us. Just by looking at the paper, I could tell that all of them were mine. Except for one, which was on purple paper. Not pastel purple paper, but purple, purple paper. The words were bleeding through the note. Written in black marker. Definitely not Charlie's handwriting. This was a note from Betsy, and I was 800 percent sure it wasn't for me.

The note was folded really tightly, with one of the edges jammed into one of the folds. It wouldn't just "accidentally" open. Believe me, I tried. I dropped it about twenty times and tapped it on the edge of my desk.

"Einstein!" I called. Moments later he raced up the stairs and joined me, toy in his mouth. "Can we switch-eroo, bud?" I asked, offering him the note in exchange for the toy, which was shaped like a piece of bacon. "Just pull on it a little?"

He wasn't going for it. He shook his toy wildly, showing off. I couldn't resist and grabbed the end of the fuzzy pork. We played for a few minutes before he got bored of my short attention span. I couldn't help but keep looking at the note.

"You could really help me out here," I reminded him.

Einstein took his toy and bounded back downstairs. A dog with scruples. With a sigh, I chucked the note into my backpack and called it a night.

I didn't sleep well, though. It was like the note was burning a hole through my bag and into my soul. What was it? Probably a love note. Oh, yuck. Is that why she didn't want to hang around? Maybe I didn't want to read that anyway. Either way, I couldn't wait to get it out of my temptation zone.

CHAPTER NINE
THE BREAKER UPPERER

I woke up as a woman on a mission. A strange and unusual mission: to track Betsy down as soon as possible. As soon as I was dressed, I plowed down the stairs and stepped into a scene I was not familiar with: Ms. Watson was with Dad in the kitchen making breakfast.

"Kiddo!" Dad greeted me.

"Hey, you two," I said, eyeing the happy duo.

"You are about to lose your mind," Dad told me, a huge smile on his face. He filled a plate with pancakes and handed it to me.

"Oh, really?"

"Can I tell her?" Dad asked Ms. Watson.

"Sure," she answered, then flipped a pancake right in the pan without using a spatula.

"Some high-up lady at school," Dad whispered, using his thumb to point at Ms. Watson, "decided you get to have today off."

"What?"

"Part of the wedding celebration!" Dad grinned at me expectantly.

I looked at Ms. Watson. This was very, very, very strange.

"With the stress of the wedding and all of the preparation you've helped with, I thought a personal day would be wise. Health-wise."

"I, uh, have a math test today," I said. It sounded better than me trying to explain how I needed to get to school to pass a note I hadn't even read that still, somehow, made me very nervous.

"That's next Friday," Ms. Watson corrected me, and pointed to a new calendar that was stuck to the front of the fridge.

I walked over and looked at it. It listed every single test. Every single appointment. Reminders for yearly physicals, furnace check-ups, and water filter change dates were there, too.

"As you can see," she continued as she filled her coffee cup, "all you have at school today is an assembly this afternoon. An ideal day for this."

"But I would be alone all day," I heard myself say. I couldn't believe I was protesting a day off of school that was being handed to me on a platter!

"I took the day off as well," Ms. Watson said. "We would be together. Then this evening we'd be all refreshed for the party."

"What's up?" Dad asked me. "I thought you'd be spouting out fireworks. Or at least doing cartwheels."

"Are you kidding?" I forced a smile. "This is amazing! But I can't."

Both Dad and Ms. Watson looked at me like I was bananas.

"I know how it sounds!" I laughed. "But there are still party favors in the art room that I need to get for tonight." That, thankfully, was true! Phew.

"We can pick them up on the way to the party," Ms. Watson decided.

"I meant there are still favors I need to *make* with the stuff in the art room." That, bummerfully, was not true.

"I'm sure we'll be just fine without them," Dad insisted.

"No, this was my responsibility. I really want to do it right," I told him. "I better hurry or I'll miss Charlie."

"I already had Rik text him that you were staying home today," Ms. Watson said.

"Oh. Well, a walk by myself won't kill me, right, Dad?"

"My little trouper," Dad said proudly.

"Seriously, Veronica, you should just stay home."

Dad and I turned to look at Ms. Watson, shocked.

"Did you just call me 'Veronica'?" I asked.

"I think I did," she said, almost as surprised as we were.

"I can't believe I'm saying this, but we can't force her to skip school," Dad said. "Go learn something!" He laughed and gave me a smooch on the head. "See you tonight, party princess."

"I'll see you tonight," I answered cheerfully as I shot out the door.

I had, indeed, missed Charlie. In fact, I had missed every-one. I barely made it to homeroom. Luckily, my fortunes improved when I went to art class. Betsy was there work-ing on one of the computers!

"Here. I got this on accident," I said as I handed her the purple treasure trove of secrets.

"You read it?" she asked.

"No. No!" I reassured her. "I definitely did not."

She grabbed my hand and put the note back in it. "Read it."

"It's for me?"

She shook her head.

"I don't understand—"

"Read it. But not in front of everyone. Come on." She gestured for me to follow her. Betsy grabbed the hall pass off the art teacher's desk and ushered me down the hall and into the girls' bathroom.

Suddenly, what I had wanted to do so badly last night was the last thing in the world I wanted to do now.

The other girls in the bathroom spotted Betsy and cleared out. Once they were out of earshot, Betsy nodded at me.

"If this is between you and Charlie, maybe I shouldn't

be involved," I suggested. My arm was still stretched out to her, and I was holding the note with just the very tips of my fingers.

She gnawed on her lip before saying, "I need your help."

"But it's folded so nicely," I said nervously, stalling for time.

She rolled her eyes and grabbed the note back, prying it completely open in a millisecond and pushing it deeply into my palm.

"There."

"Betsy, I don't know if I'm comfortable with this. In fact, I'm not."

She looked at the floor and let out an annoyed sigh. "Please?" she mumbled.

That's when I turned into a giant jack-in-the box and bobbed wildly around the room on my giant spring. Okay, so that didn't happen, but I liked to think that is what *would* have happened if I still had my powers. I was that surprised to hear Betsy say *please*.

"Uh, okay," I said as I pulled at the edges of the note, smoothing it out. "Do you want me to read it out loud?"

"No. Definitely not," she said. Then Betsy turned away from me and began pacing.

Okay, Veri, prepare to be grossed out, I told myself. But as I started reading, my heart sank. This wasn't a love note. It was a heartbreaker note. Betsy was telling him she didn't like him the way he liked her.

"Oh," I said quietly. "That's why things were so weird at ice cream."

"Yeah," Betsy answered. "I thought he had gotten the note and just hadn't read it yet. It wasn't until later when Charlie was all . . . Charlie . . . that I realized you had gotten it instead."

It was definitely a letter written by Betsy. And I use the term *letter* loosely. It was only three sentences:

Sorry, dude. I only want to be friends. That's all.

Betsy looked at me with hopeful eyes. "So?"

"It's a little harsh," I admitted.

"But I said 'sorry,'" Betsy explained.

"Yeah, but you didn't tell him why or anything."

"I don't think he's cute," she said bluntly.

"Hmm. Okay, maybe don't lead with that."

"Well, I mean, he's cute like my little brother is cute. Also annoying like him. Should I have said that?"

"No. Definitely don't do that either. Just talk to him like . . . like . . ." I struggled for a comparison.

"Like I was you?" Betsy interrupted.

"For lack of better a word, yes."

"Why did he have to go there? Things were fine between us. More than fine!" she said in an octave higher than I'd ever heard her use. "I'm not good at this stuff like you, Veronica."

"I'm not 'good' at this stuff!" I told her. Really, what was this vibe I was giving off? First Charlie wanted help wooing, then Betsy wanted help breaking.

She finally stopped pacing and looked up at me, a steely darkness in her eyes.

"*You* are gonna tell him, weirdo."

It was a tone I hadn't heard in a while, but one I knew very well. Unfortunately, this time, despite the primal fear it stabbed into my guts, I couldn't give in.

I tiptoed backward a few feet before telling her, "I can't, Betsy. I won't. Even if you beat me up. I can't do this to Charlie."

She stepped toward me and I instinctively put my arms up in an X to cover my face.

"I'm sorry, I'm sorry!" I cried out.

"Dude! Chill!" she said. "I wasn't going to hit you."

Slowly I lowered my arms until I could get a peek at her. She didn't look mad. She actually looked sad.

Betsy shook her head. "After everything we've been through the past few months, you think I would do that?"

I slid my arms down my sides. "Old habits, I guess."

"I, um, I'm sorry, Veronica. I'm not used to the whole 'friend' thing," she confessed. "Or, really, the 'apologizing' thing either."

"It's okay," I told her.

"I'm sorry," she repeated. "That's why all of this with Charlie is so hard. It took forever just for me to write I was sorry in the note. And I just want to be friends! It's a disaster."

I couldn't help but feel bad for her. But, honestly, I was a little happy for me. True, it was terrible that Charlie was going to get knocked back, but that was always gonna happen, right? It's not like they were meant to be! Like they were going to get married one day or something! We could let him down in the most gentle, humane way possible, and then I'd get my Charlie back. Decision made.

"I'll help you. I won't tell Charlie for you, but I'll help you tell him in the best way you can."

"Thank you," she said, relieved. "Again, I'm super sorry."

"You can probably stop apologizing now." I chuckled.

"It's kind of addictive. Sort of takes some weight off your shoulders. It's freeing. I'm sorry, Veronica!"

"Okay, please stop now. We have work to do."

"I'm sorry I delayed the work because of my apologies." She was hamming it up now.

"Betsy!"

"Sorry!"

We went back to art class and did a very un-art-class thing: We wrote a breakup letter for a relationship that never even happened.

"Holy cow," Betsy rasped. "That's amazing. It's like what I'm feeling, but in words."

I nodded. It was a pretty good letter, for something you use to destroy the heart of a young man. I had been careful to not use any cliché things like, "It's not you, it's me," even if that one was pretty applicable. Instead I stuck to facts but smooshed a lot of flattery in with them. I don't know what that would be called. Let's call it *flac-*

terry. Charlie was amazing. True. Betsy wasn't ready for a relationship. True. Betsy respected him so much that she wanted to always be friends and not risk ruining it with an attempt at dating. Flacterry. But most importantly, he needed to know that she'd always be there for him no matter what he said or did. Flacterry for Betsy, fact for me. Not gonna lie, writing it had made me a bit more emotional than I had anticipated. Though is that really something you can anticipate? I hope having to write a heartbreaker note to your best friend for your former enemy isn't a standard middle-school thing.

"Do you feel that?" Lizzie asked everyone.

"That misty feeling?" Dean answered.

"Yeah. It's like we're in the misty mountains or something."

I held my hand out to feel the air. It did feel a little damp.

"Might be something's up with the cleaning station?" Betsy suggested.

"Oh, yeah, it has that misty sanitizer thing," I remembered.

Lizzie nodded in agreement and went back to sculpting an eyeball.

A few minutes later the bell rang.

"You'll be ready?" Betsy asked as we were about to head our separate ways.

"Yeah, but don't tell him I already knew."

"I won't."

I wished I could leave a stupidmessage for Charlie today, but all I could do was wait. I knew Betsy was giving him the note near the end of the day, but who could be sure when he would actually read it? It was a rather torturous day, to be honest, but when I went to get my backpack to go meet my mom, I knew it had happened. Charlie was slumped into his locker. Like, literally *into* his locker. No sight of his head whatsoever.

You don't know. You don't know, I reminded myself as I walked up to him.

"Hey, what up, bud?" I said in a waaaaaaaaay too cheery voice.

"Umph."

"You okay?" I asked as I moved over to my locker and got my stuff out.

He pulled himself out of his locker. His face was red and a little puffy.

"You aren't okay. Come on." I grabbed both of our backpacks and guided him back to the art room. The scene of the crime. It felt strange to take him there, but it was the only place I knew would be deserted. Plus, I had to pick up my party favors.

As weirdness would have it, Charlie sat down right in the same seat where Betsy had sat while we wrote the note. I sat next to him, exactly where I had sat with Betsy.

I didn't want to start, so I put my hand on his shoulder and gave it a little squeeze.

He let out a deep breath and then said, "Betsy doesn't like me."

I was still getting my bearings.

"She doesn't like me like *that*, I mean," he added. Probably because of my silence.

"Oh. I'm so sorry."

"Like, I get it, all right, I've seen my share of romcoms. Sometimes it's just not there or whatever, that's not her fault, but it's . . . it's . . ." He trailed off.

"It's what?"

"It's bloody embarrassing! Everyone's gonna know now."

"Yeah," I agreed.

"Veri!"

"So what if they do?"

"It will be sooo embarrassing!"

"Well," I said, still thinking it through, "we know they will know. There isn't anything we can do about that."

Charlie plopped his forehead onto the table.

"But," I added, "why should you care? It's not fair to have to fake what's going on with you just to save face or whatever."

"That sounds like Rik advice." His voice was muffled.

Ew. He was right.

"Well, it's probably good advice then. Hard, infuriating advice, but good advice."

"If things are cool with Betsy, then what does it matter?"

"Things aren't cool with Bets."

"Are you sure? I'd assume she still really wants to be friends with you. Do you—"

Charlie flung his head back up and interrupted me. "Do I want to build a time machine and go back and never tell her any of the stuff I told her? Why, yes. Yes I do."

"Oh, Charlie, I wish we could. At least things can go back to being normal. She can be our distant friend and all that."

"I don't want to be distant friends with her, Veri!" he said, upset. "She is our friend. And she cares about you a lot!"

"Sorry," I said. "I was just trying to cheer you up."

"It's okay." He sighed. "What do I say to her now? Talk about awkward." Charlie let out an epic groan. "At least I have the weekend and won't see her for a bit."

I cringed. "Party tonight."

"Ahh!" Charlie tipped his chair completely over, falling to the floor dramatically. Luckily, it made us both laugh.

"Remind me to never like anyone ever again, okay?" he said, looking up at me.

"Roger that."

"Wanna stop off somewhere on our way home and stuff our faces?"

"I wish I could. I'm . . ." I stopped.

"Yes?"

"I'm meeting my mom."

Charlie sighed. "You're lucky I am emotionally drained. I can't even fight with you about that."

Speaking of which, I knew I was about to be super late for meeting her.

"Will you be okay for the next hour or so?" I asked. "We'll figure it out. I promise. I'll even be there when you talk to Betsy if you want."

"I'm just going to wallow here for a little while," he said, covering his face with his arms.

"On the floor?"

"Yep. Maybe it will open up and suck me in."

"I'll see you at six, okay?" I gently shook his arm.

Charlie lifted one elbow, so I could see an eye.

"You'll really be okay?" I asked.

"Yes. Will you?"

"Of course. It's my mom," I said, rolling my eyes.

"Remember me . . . ," Charlie crackled, pretending to die as I walked out of the art room.

I was so relieved to see Mom's SUV waiting on the corner. She was inside, puffing intently on a cigarette. I walked up and went to open the passenger-side door, but it was locked, so I knocked on the window. She rolled the window down.

"So?" she asked without looking at me.

"I'm sorry I'm late. There was this thing with Charlie . . ."

"Get in," she instructed. "We are *way* behind schedule."

Once I was buckled in and we were driving, I didn't know what to say. Mom lit a new cigarette with the last bit of the old one. It wasn't like her to smoke in front of me. I knew Dad would have a lot of questions if I came home smelling like smoke, but I was too scared to ask her to put it out. She looked really mad, so I decided I would just be quiet. Sometimes when Dad got upset, he needed to take a few minutes to collect himself. And sometimes he suggested I do the same. We ended up driving all the way to her apartment without saying a word. After she parked, we both sat in the steely silence without moving.

Finally, she turned to look at me and let out a puff of smoke. "Maybe this was a bad idea."

"What?" I said quietly.

"Us. Trying to act normal when we can't even keep our promises to meet at specific times. I'm sure you are still keeping all of this from your father?"

"Just for now," I told her. "I thought things were going really well. Very normal. I don't have my powers anymore and we get along great. I think. And since things are changing at Dad's house so much and you and I haven't gotten a lot of time together over the years . . . well, I was hoping I could maybe come live with you?"

She looked stunned. "Live with me?"

I held my breath.

CHAPTER TEN
THE POWERS THAT BE

"I noticed you have a spare room," I said sheepishly to my mom. "If you don't like the way Dad is raising me, then maybe you could start doing it instead?"

I felt my chin tremble, so I bit my lip to stabilize it. It was a hard thing to say. I didn't think Dad was doing a bad job raising me. I really didn't. And Mom's disapproval of him really rubbed me the wrong way, but . . . but. Big freaking but. What else could I do? Dad didn't need me anymore, and going with Mom would be my first, and probably only, shot at being normal. I wanted to believe this other stuff between the two of them could be worked out and that they could be civil to each other. That's all

I was hoping for, not friendship or getting back together like people do in movies.

Bzz! Bzz!

"Seriously? Does your phone ever stop?" she said, annoyed.

I took a quick look at the screen. I was supposed to be home with Dad, prepping for his bachelor party. "Who's ready to Par-tayyy?" his text read, along with a pic of Einstein wearing a very snazzy dog bowtie.

"I mean," I continued, "now that I don't have powers anymore we could live together and it would be a normal thing. A normal life. It seems like that's what you want, too."

She stared at me for a moment.

"No," she finally answered.

"Why not?" I asked quietly.

She shrugged her shoulders before saying, "I dunno. I have a lot going on. Not sure if motherhood is for me."

I couldn't believe it. Was she really saying this? "But you are my mom."

"Genetically," she agreed.

Now the tears were really trying to force their way out of my eyes. I held my breath, trying to will them not to emerge, but that had started to make me light-headed.

She continued, "Having a teenager in your life? That's a big commitment. It's not like you're a cute little baby or something." My mom kept on talking, but my brain was starting to go elsewhere.

Her words were digging into me, gutting me. She didn't want to be my mom. After all this, she didn't want me. I felt hollow.

"Ahh!!" my mother screamed, bringing me out of my thoughts.

She was staring at me. A look of extreme panic was etched on her pale face.

"What? Wait, did I hit the seat adjuster or something?" I asked. It seemed I was looking up at her now.

I felt the side of the seat, but it was fine.

"Y-you liar!" My mom's panic had turned into something worse: disgust. She pointed at my waist.

I looked down, trying to figure out what she could be so upset about. I wasn't even wearing a sassy T-shirt. Then, I saw it.

No, no, no, I thought. *This can't be happening.*

"This can't be happening!" I said.

Much to everyone's surprise, my stupidpowers had activated. I was starting to shrink, but I didn't feel smaller;

I felt heavier. Looking down, I could see the horrible truth. The soles of my shoes were spreading outward. The rejection from my mom had left me feeling empty, which sparked my powers to make it appear like I actually was empty. I looked like I was melting.

"Get. Out," she commanded.

"I didn't lie," I tried to explain. "They told me I was cured—"

"Sure! And your guardian angel coming to threaten me this afternoon? I'm sure you didn't know about that either."

"What? Betsy?" I was so confused.

"None of it matters now. Your secret is out. This is not normal." She gestured to my wobbly torso.

"Please," I begged. "I just want to live with you. I just want us to be normal."

She pointed to the door. And that was all it took. Devastation swept over me, and I felt an extra-special second wave of stupidpowers starting. I turned to get out of the car, trying to escape before my mother witnessed another freak show, but the jiggliness of my upper body was making it hard to move at any reasonable speed. Plus, there was this extraordinary heaviness in my heart that seemed to be dragging my whole body down.

"Hurry! Get your mess out of my car!" my mother demanded.

It was then that the powers went into high gear, and so did the melting process.

The jelly-ness of my belly was now a cute memory. I was rapidly getting shorter and wider. Flatter and rounder? Yep. That too. Finally, my mother reached over and opened the car door for me. She was about to push my globulous self out of her SUV when she thought better.

"Yuck," she said, then rifled around in the back seat until she found a snow brush/ice-scraper thingy. Using the dingy blue sweeper side, she brushed me out of the car. I stuck about halfway through and she had to employ the scraper side.

"That's uncomfortable," I told her as she pried what had been my left elbow off the seat.

"This is unacceptable, Veronica," she hissed.

A second later, I splatted onto the curb. My mother slammed the door and took off. Her wheels screeched as she peeled out. I needed to get myself together. I was a gelatinous, roughly girl-shaped blob that was hanging out on the sidewalk! With a lot of effort, I dragged my gooey bits behind a nearby hedge. I closed my eyes and took a few deep breaths before trying to assess the sitch. My mother hated me. I was an actual mess. A few more breaths and the powers were starting to wear off, but I still wasn't anywhere near back to normal. The hedges were taller than me and I had an overall gummy bear–like appearance. Not to mention my butt kept getting stuck to the grass. I lifted my hand to inspect it, but noticed it had a mini candy bar wrapper stuck to it. I plucked it off only to see that there was a large crow's feather stuck to my ankle. That one was really stuck.

As I slowly returned more and more to my natural self, I could see that the wrapper and feather were the least of my sticky problems. My whole body was covered with grass clippings, litter, and even a few bugs. Once I was stable enough to walk, I could only hope they'd fall off as I made my way home.

SPLAT! STICK! SPLOOP!
SPLAT! STICK! SPLOOP!
SPLAT! STICK! SPLOOP!

That was my lovely, limby soundtrack all the way home. My feet hadn't quite recovered and stuck to the sidewalk on Every. Single. Step. I was so late getting home that there were already party guests arriving!

"Dad! I'm here!" I called out as I burst through the door. "Wow . . . ," I said. All of my decorations had been put up, and they looked great! I peeked into the living room and spotted Charlie, who was taping up the last bit of streamer. He wasn't looking at it, though; his eyes were focused on the other side of the room. Betsy. She was working with Lizzie and Dean to get the fancy video camera ready. At that moment, her head shot up and she looked over at Charlie. Even from this distance I could see how red his face turned. Betsy whipped her head back to Lizzie and Dean, pretending it had never happened.

I wanted to hug both of them.

But that would've been really gross. I had just remembered I was still crawling with actual, living bugs.

"Kiddo! We're in the kitchen!" Dad called out. I could tell by the voices that some of his dude friends had already arrived.

"I'll be right there! Just gonna go change!" I said too loudly, hoping Dad would think I didn't hear him. I raced up the stairs, but stopped abruptly on the landing. Ms. Watson was standing there staring at me.

"Hi," I said, flashing a big fake smile.

"What happened to you?" she asked as she gently picked a ladybug out of my hair and set it on our fern.

"Oh, well . . . nothing."

"Powers?" she asked quietly.

"Yeah. I'm fine, though," I assured her as I slid past.

SNIFF-SNIFF!

Did Ms. Watson just sniff me? Whatever. I needed a moment when no one else could see me. Once I was safely inside the bathroom with the door locked behind me, I inspected the damage. Yep. I was encased in ick. There were sticks nestled under my armpits and moss on my kneecaps. I sat on the edge of the tub and ran the water. I didn't have a ton of time—the party would be in full swing soon—so a scrub with a washcloth would have to be enough for this deforestation.

I began the process of soaking and scrubbing, soaking and scrubbing. It was super monotonous, so I started making a mental list of what still needed done for tomorrow. The portrait! I needed to give that to them that night. I hoped they would like it, and not just an "oh, this is nice" kind of like. It was the hardest I'd ever worked on a drawing.

There was a *tap-tap-tap* coming from the floor below—Dad's personal Morse Code for "You're wasting water."

"Oh, crud," I mumbled, realizing I had totally zoned out. Now that I was more human than roadside debris, I got ready in a flash, grabbed the portrait, and ran downstairs.

The rooms were filling up with people I had known my entire life, some of whom I hadn't seen since I was a wee baby. It was really trippy. I should have counted how many times I heard, "Veronica?! Is that you? You've gotten so big!" My guess would be at least twenty-two million times. Eventually I dropped off my portrait, wrapped and decorated with the most enormous bow I could make, next to the fireplace.

It took longer than expected, but then I found Charlie. "Thank you for doing all of this!" I marveled at the decorations.

"At your service." He bowed. "But, actually, I needed something to keep me busy. It took me ages to get off the art room floor."

I gasped. His comment had set off a reminder.

"The favors!" I had left them at school!

"Chill your grill," Charlie said as he pointed to my dad's friends Waldo and Frank, who were popping a cracker open. "I brought them."

"You are a real American hero."

"A real American zero, you mean."

His face fell a little as he snuck a glance at Betsy.

"Wanna go talk to her?" I asked.

He shook his head violently.

"Okay."

This was tricky. Really tricky. Part of me—and I acknowledge how not cool it is to say this—but part of me was a little happy. There. I said it. I'm a horrible human being. Charlie was my best friend again. I could still be friends with Betsy in that weird way we were friends. Things could go back to the way they were. Well, except that one thing . . .

"Oh. You need to tell your moms something. Something not good."

Charlie's eyes widened. "Side effects? Itching? Burning? Flaking? Organ prolapse?!"

"It stopped working. I'm powered up again."

"Yes!" He rejoiced before correcting himself. "I mean, so sorry to hear that, love. How bad?"

I had had a bad itch behind one ear since I came downstairs and had a sneaking suspicion of what it was.

"One hundred percent bad," I answered, pulling my hair to the side so Charlie could take a look.

"Is that part of a funny from a newspaper?" He picked at it. "What happened?"

"I was a human Jell-O mold."

"This is gross. Beautifully gross," he said in awe as he pulled out the stuck comic strip.

"Which comic is it?" I asked.

"Looks like a panel from Garfield."

Charlie took a picture of the comic and texted it to his moms with an update about my power surge.

It only took a few minutes for them to write back.

"Hey, they say they can make you more. Sounds like it would be like a vitamin you have to take every so often to keep your powers away."

"Okay. Gummy bear me."

"You sure about this?" Charlie asked, his thumbs looming over his phone screen.

"Yeah."

Charlie hesitated before typing his response. "Order placed."

I could see that Dad had noticed the giant-bowed gift. It wouldn't be long until he couldn't resist anymore.

"I should get Betsy and the twins. Make sure they're

filming." I gestured to the crowd that was gathering. "Wanna come with me?"

"Nah. I'll, uh, hold down this corner of the room," Charlie said.

Betsy and the twins had really gotten into their jobs. Betsy was filming guests from dramatic angles while they told her about how they knew Dad or Ms. Watson. The Tech Twins were prepping the next video well-wishers, smoothing down fly-aways, and adjusting lighting. I waited until they were between spots to bother them.

"You three are blowing my mind!"

"If you're going to do it . . . ," Lizzie started.

"Do it well," Dean finished.

"Yo," Betsy said, "your dad knows some interesting-looking characters."

I couldn't help but laugh. He did. In fact, he had one friend I only knew as Fist Face. He was from Dad's rough-and-tumble phase, so I had never asked if it was because his face looked like a fist or if it was because he used his fists a lot. On faces. Some questions you just shouldn't ask.

Lizzie nodded. "I feel like there is a subject of a documentary in here."

The twins went back to prep.

"So, how is he?" Betsy asked me quietly.

"Embarrassed," I said.

"That's lame."

"Maybe you should break the ice?" I asked.

"I tried to go talk to him, but he kept running away."

"I'm sure it wasn't on purpose. Maybe he didn't notice you."

"No, he literally saw me. Then I waved. Then he ran away. Blew napkins off the table he was going so fast."

"Oof."

"I dunno. I ruined it. I'm just going to let it go."

Again, I was conflicted. Sharing Charlie was not my favorite thing.

Tink-tink-tink!

We turned to see my dad, who was tapping a butter knife on the side of a beer mug.

"Where's Veronica? Where are you at, kiddo?"

"We're on!" I whispered to Betsy and the twins.

I joined Dad and Ms. Watson by the fireplace. The guests had gathered around.

"I take it this is your doing?" Dad asked as he lifted the package onto the edge of a coffee table.

"I know it's tradition to give the bride and groom something on the wedding day, but . . . this was way too frickin' big to haul to the mansion," I kidded.

"Can we open it tonight?" he asked hopefully.

"Yeah," I said nervously. Suddenly I wasn't sure my art was any good at all. "I mean, maybe . . ." I reached toward the present, but it was too late; Dad the Present Annihilator ripped off the wrapping paper in the blink of an eye and stood silent before the canvas. Several of the guests gasped.

Panic bolted up my spine. I could feel my powers starting to churn. My eyes darted between him and Ms. Watson, trying to gauge their feelings before mine reached the point of no return.

Dad turned to me. He had tears in his eyes.

"Veri, this is amazing!" Dad beamed at me. "I knew you were impressive, but this . . . THIS!" He picked me up and spun me around before planting a big fat kiss on my forehead.

I let out a huge sigh of relief and an even huger one when I felt my powers taper off.

"It is stunning," Ms. Watson said. "Thank you."

The rest of the adult guests gathered around the canvas

to get a better look while I slid back into the group of kids. Charlie had gotten brave and was within talking range of Betsy, but neither of them would even look at the other.

"Way to show us all up, weirdo," Betsy joked.

"I'll take that as the highest compliment," I told her.

"You probably should."

"Just one thing, Veri," Charlie added. "Why aren't you in it? Family portrait and all that."

I watched Dad and Ms. Watson, their arms wrapped around each other. They were in their own little world.

"I guess it didn't look right."

A little while later, the guests were starting to mill out, but I was waiting for one in particular.

"Ted!" I called out as his head bobbed toward the front door.

"What up, little dunk?" he asked.

I wasn't at all sure what a *little dunk* was, but I had more important things to discuss. And I wanted to do it before I lost my nerve.

"Uh," I stammered. "I need to ask you another favor."

"As long as you don't need me to pee in a cup for you, consider it done."

"Oh, no, I don't know why—"

"I mean, I would normally, but I just peed like two minutes ago, so I'm running on empty."

"Oh, boy. No, Ted, what I need is for you to tell my mom that I'm fine now. And I'm going to be fine from now on. I can even get professionals to tell her that. I'm done with all that weird stuff."

He scrunched his brow. "And you're sure you don't need to pass a drug test?"

"More than anything in the world, I don't need you to pee in a cup for me. Please tell my mom that. Please."

"All right . . ."

"Soon! Please."

Ted nodded as he left, though he still looked extremely confused.

Might be time to put myself in a new picture.

CHAPTER ELEVEN
FOREVER AND NEVER

Wedding day! Aaaaaand I was already running late. I was supposed to have met Ms. Watson fifteen minutes earlier. But. *But* I had seen a puppy. *You* try to resist a ball of mushy fluff!

I rushed into the Dress Depot and found Ms. Watson—well, at least her feet and hair. She was in the dressing room trying on her wedding dress.

"Ms. Watson! I'm here! I'm so sorry!" I said through the curtain.

"Your stuff is in the next changing room," she instructed.

"Did we get Dad's suit?" I asked as I closed myself into the dressing room.

"Yep."

"When does he try his on to make sure it fits?"

"Leave it to the patriarchy to make all men's sizes to be in their actual measurements whereas our sizes are a mere guideline. He won't even need to take his out of the dry-cleaning bag until two minutes before the ceremony."

I unwrapped my outfit. It had taken me ages to pick it out. The dress I had ordered was tea length, which meant it hit at about the middle of my calf. It was made out of about a zillion layers of different pastel-colored tulle. It was gloriously dramatic. I wriggled into it before I left the dressing room to show Ms. Watson.

"Maid of honor reporting for duty!" I called into her changing stall.

A few seconds later she came out of her own, and . . .

"Wow . . . ," I said. She looked great. Before, I had thought the sleek, off-the-shoulder dress she had picked out was too plain, but seeing it on her now, it was perfect.

"This is adequate?" she asked nervously.

"It's more than adequate! You're a total baberella!"

A little color came to her cheeks before she turned the

attention to me. "Your outfit is very clever. Very you. I like it quite a bit."

"Thanks," I said. There were a lot of emotions flowing through me right then. Here I was, about to be maid of honor and best man to two people I was not going to live with soon. She looked at herself in the mirror and gave a small, hesitant smile. Then she looked at my reflection.

"You are going to be a great best man, too."

Just as she said that, I spotted a small tuxedo coat on the rack with purple lapels.

"Oh. Em. Gee."

I ripped it off its hanger and slid it on. It fit perfectly.

"I'm thinking. I'm best man and maid of honor," I explained to Ms. Watson. "It's only fair that I split my outfit duties, too, right?"

"If you look that good, you kind of have to," she admitted.

"Thanks," I said, offering her a curtsy.

The seamstress had to add an extra snap to the back of Ms. Watson's dress, so we waited while she worked.

"How's everything with Charles?" Ms. Watson asked. "You two seemed to be having fun last night. Whereas he and Betsy didn't speak even once."

"You noticed?"

"Of course."

"She doesn't want to be his girlfriend, which she told him."

"And how'd he take that?"

"The right way, I guess? He wasn't mad at her or anything. Just really embarrassed."

"Ah."

"But now they are both weird about talking to each other."

"And you've offered to aid in bridging that gap, naturally," she said as if it were a fact. Not a question. A fact.

I did my best not to squirm.

"You didn't?" she said, surprised at my involuntary squirminess.

"I did at first," I confessed. "I'm not *trying* to keep them apart." I could feel the backlog of conflicting thoughts breaking free and making a run for my mouth. "It's just that he is *my* friend and then sometimes—*sometimes*—I think that maybe I like him as more than that. But then he does something extra annoying and I'm like 'No way, pal. Not ever.' But then why am I so bleh about him even being friends with Betsy?!"

Much like in my bedroom a few days ago, Ms. Watson suddenly went stiff. Then she started to stand up, but only got a few inches out of the chair before she sat back down. She swallowed hard and looked back to me. There was a shadow of fear in her eyes.

"They are both your friends?" she finally said.

I paused. "Yes."

"Then it's your duty to do your best by them," Ms. Watson instructed. "People we care about don't always do what we want, but that doesn't mean we can control them. Only mitigate the bad and help where we can."

"Hmm."

The seamstress returned with the alterations, saving me from having to actually comment on Watson's mission statement.

Ms. Watson looked at her watch. "We should probably just get changed here and go."

"Is it really that late?" I gasped. It was!

"It's all under control," Ms. Watson assured me. "Besides, it's not like they can start without us."

I pulled my dress back on and carried the tuxedo jacket to the car. I could wrangle my hair on the way. Already I felt like a hot mess, but in seconds Ms. Watson had emerged from her changing room looking posh and calm. Somehow, she had even managed to get her hair into a perfect, old-school French twist. She climbed into the car.

"Off we go."

We drove over to the church in silence as I rolled my hair into a loose bun on the top of my head. A few curls popped out here and there, so I put a little pomade on them to give them definition. I thought they looked perfect with the overall fluffiness of my dress. Plus, it made me look super busy. Too busy to talk, even. The silence felt awkward, but I should have enjoyed it because at the church everything became very, very loud.

"We need to get you inside!" I told Ms. Watson as we pulled into a parking space. There were guests walking into the church already.

"Let's find your father," she said, opening the car door.

"Have you never seen a wedding movie?! You can't see each other before the wedding! It's bad luck."

She looked at me like I was bananas.

"It's tradition?" I tried.

She grumbled, but I managed to usher her into a small room outside the main chapel. Next, speaking of ushers, I ran into a very dapper one on my way to find my dad.

"Charlie! You look great!" I said. He was wearing a real tuxedo with tails and everything.

"So do you!" He pointed at my dress.

"Have you seen my dad?"

"Yeah, he's in the chapel already. At least, I think it's a chapel. Hard to see," he said with a twinkle in his eye.

"What?"

"Come on." He led me down the hall and through the doorway.

"Whoa," I whispered.

The entire room was filled with flowers. Like, *filled*. Charlie had been right; you could barely see the walls! The only bare spot was the gift table, which was overflowing with presents. Above it hung the portrait I had drawn for them. Guess it's not too big to lug around if you're a big lug like my dad.

"See, not too many flowers," a voice boomed from behind me.

"Dad! It's breathtaking!"

"Glad ya made it." He winked at me. "We about ready to rock?"

I nodded.

"Cool. I'll make sure everyone is settled." He went on

a hand-shaking tour through the rows of seats. Almost all of them were already full.

"Nervous?" Charlie asked me.

"A little, but I'm not sure why."

"Oh! That reminds me." Charlie dug around in his pockets until he produced a tiny sandwich bag. "They made a bunch but want to give them to you one at a time 'cause they think you'll have to take a new one every week or so."

I took the baggie from him. In it was one solitary gummy bear.

"Thank you!" I said as I stuffed it into my jacket pocket.

"You aren't going to take it right now?" Charlie asked.

"Maybe in a minute," I told him. Something else had caught my attention. "There's the twins . . . and Betsy."

Charlie blew a raspberry and started walking away. "Smell ya later."

Betsy spotted me and waved frantically.

"Wait, Charlie, something's up."

We rushed over to her.

"Uh, um." Betsy's eyes darted around nervously at the sight of Charlie.

Charlie made an odd ticking noise and looked at his shoes.

"What is it?" I asked her.

She snapped out of it, remembering why she had waved me over in the first place.

Betsy leaned in to whisper, "Your mom is here."

Surprise, followed by primal panic, surged through my veins. It was too late. A little stupidpower made a small, happy daisy spring from the palm of my hand. Instinctively, Charlie and Betsy crowded around me so no one else could see. Pretty much instantly, though, the petals burst into flames and burnt the whole thing to soot.

That couldn't be a good sign.

"Where?!" I tried to whisper, but it came out as more of a whisper-scream.

Betsy nodded out the door toward the parking lot. One would think that was too general of a direction, but as soon as I stepped outside, I spotted her. She was wearing one of those hat-type things that British people wear to weddings. A fascinator. If you've never heard of them, look them up. You'll probably see a picture of my mother in her fascinator because it was the Mother of All Fascinators.

"Her hat looks just like the mobile that used to hang over my brother's crib," Betsy observed.

It *was* rather mobile-like. There was a central hat. Red. It was only about the size of a teacup, though. Four red antennae, each about two feet long, arched out of it. Each had a feather-covered orb dangling off its tip. From the front hung a sheer red veil that covered my mother's left eye and nose.

"Fascinating!" Charlie nudged me with his elbow.

Both Betsy and I gave him dirty looks for that horrible joke.

"Sorry."

She was here. That's what I had wanted. Originally, at least. But now that she was *really* here and heading toward us at an alarming pace, I had the very bad feeling this was a horrible idea. Maybe she wanted me now. Maybe she had thought it over and felt really guilty! Maybe she would come in and make amends and take me back with her to her figurine-filled abode and I could start again. Normal life. I rushed to the entryway to cut her off. The outside door led into a little room of its own, which was studded with beautiful stained-glass windows that peered into the main room. There were double doors on each of the far ends of the wall leading into the main room. I was grateful. This would give me a buffer to talk to Mom before she went in.

"Hi!" I greeted her cheerfully as she strutted in.

She took a step back once she noticed me. "Hello."

"Wow, um, thanks for coming."

"Ted told me you were really better now. Something about proof?"

"Uh, yeah. Hold on." I fumbled around in my pocket.

"Nope!" My dad's voice cut through the peaceful classical music that was playing through the speaker system. "You need to not be here." Dad had spotted the hat and the lady and had left the main room of the church to join us at the front of the building. He was clearly going to take absolutely zero time in kicking her out.

"Nice to see you, too, Rik," my mother answered.

"You weren't invited. Out."

"Oh, but I was. Our dear daughter was kind enough to think of me."

Dad put his hand to his forehead. "Veri . . ."

I looked around. The other room was full and the wedding was supposed to have started already. People were starting to stare. Even Charlie and Betsy had backed up to give us space.

"Dad," I said quietly, trying to shift our rather noticeable little group out of sight, "Just let her stay. Let's be adults about this."

"Yeah," my mother agreed. "Besides, you should get used to it. She's coming to live with me."

Dad chortled.

"True story," she added. "In fact, it was her idea."

Dad's amusement turned into confusion. He looked at me, realizing that my mother wasn't lying. His brow slowly furrowed as he tried to make sense of it. "What?" he finally said, as if he hadn't heard her right.

"I thought that since you and Ms. Watson were starting a new life that maybe . . . I dunno, maybe I should, too. I don't know how I fit in anymore." That last little bit stung as it came out of my mouth. It was almost like I didn't know how true it felt until I said it.

Dad's expression fell. "Veri, no," he said gently as he crouched down to look me straight in the eye. "No. Our family—"

"She made her choice, Rik," my mother interrupted.

Dad shot back up. "You. You need to go. Now." He put his hand up into the air, which accidentally signaled Fist Face to start playing the bridal march!

I stuck my head through the entryway into the main room. Ms. Watson had just entered, but when she noticed that no one else was there, she looked to the back of the room, leaning over to see through one of the doorways. Her small smile turned right upside down when she saw what was happening at the back of the room. She motioned for Fist Face to stop the music. There was a lot of murmuring coming from the crowd.

"Stay in your seats!" Ms. Watson told them calmly but firmly. "This will just take a moment."

"If it isn't the guardian angel," my mother said dryly when Ms. Watson marched up to us. "I thought you'd had enough of me already."

"Already?" Dad asked.

"Oh, this one paid me a visit a few days ago. Told me to stay away from my own daughter."

"It was you?" I looked at Ms. Watson for an explanation, but she didn't even attempt to give one.

"I don't care what you think is going on here, but this is neither the place nor the time," Ms. Watson told her.

Dad let out a shallow breath. "Veri has decided she wants to go live with her," he told Ms. Watson.

Finally, Ms. Watson turned her head sharply to look at me. For the first time ever, I saw hurt in her eyes.

"I'm not explaining it right. It's not coming out the way it should . . . ," I tried to tell them.

Ms. Watson didn't take her eyes off me as she asked my mother the next question. "And you've changed your mind about Veronica's abilities, have you? You no longer think they make her a freak?"

I looked at my feet. "Everyone says things they don't mean sometimes."

"And she's assured me the freaky stuff is done," my mother explained. "Cured, I believe."

"How did you expect to keep that lie going?" Dad asked me.

Oh boy. "It wasn't a lie."

Now both Dad and Ms. Watson looked at me, aghast.

"But last night . . . ," Ms. Watson said.

"I, uh, Lucia and Dr. Weathers made me something. It . . . helps. I just have to take it every so often. Like a flu shot." I fought the impulse to pull the gummy bear out of my pocket. I had a feeling it wouldn't help my argument.

"There are so many things wrong here." Dad sounded defeated.

"Oh, please, Rik . . . ," my mother grumbled.

"Don't even start with me," he warned her.

"You are not at all equipped to care for Veronica," Ms. Watson stated.

"You don't get to tell me anything about *my* daughter!" my mother shouted. That was the snapping point. All the adults started yelling at each other at the same time. People waiting for the wedding were craning their necks to see what all the noise was about. I went to the doorway closest to me and pulled the doorstop out. As the door closed, I saw Betsy run to Fist Face and tell him something. Seconds later, as I was closing the other double door, the classical music was blaring through the sound system at ten times the volume it originally was. It blocked out the yelling. And possibly damaged some eardrums. From where I was standing, though, I could hear everything they were saying.

"You only want her if she is cured!"

"You're a monster for keeping her this way!"

"I can't believe you'd do this. No, actually I can. Especially today."

Things were starting to get fuzzy. I don't mean fuzzy warm or fuzzy cozy. My vision was starting to go fuzzy and it felt like I was swaying from side to side. I'd never been seasick, but I imagined this was exactly what it was like. The arguing continued.

"What does that mean?"

"It means exactly what you think it does. This doesn't have anything to do with Veri. This is all about you! Just like everything always was!"

Suddenly I was jerked to one side, toward my mom. I assumed she had pulled me by my elbow, but she wasn't even looking at me. She was still deep in it with Dad and Ms. Watson. Then, again, I was yanked in the other direction. The force was strong enough to make my head flop to the side. Suddenly I realized what was happening, but it was too late.

Yank! "You both need to stop!" Ms. Watson tried to cut through their argument but was more focused on me. "Veronica?!"

"She's fine!" my mother screeched. *Fling!*

"Does she look fine?!"

Spoiler alert: I didn't.

My powers had reared their ugly head in an epic-event kinda way. I felt so unsure and conflicted about my parents that I was literally being pulled side to side depending on their argument. The bigger problem was that now that I was in the midst of it, I couldn't control it or calm it down. As I got more upset, I was being tugged harder and faster until I was thrashing across the room. Dad grabbed my arms and tried to hold me still.

"Veri?!" I heard Charlie's panicked voice cry out.

"Chuck! Pull the fire alarm before anyone sees her!" Dad instructed him. "Make them go out the other way!"

"Ah!" I cried out in pain. My dad was strong, but my powers were stronger. They'd break my arms off if he didn't let go.

"You are why she's like this!" my mother hissed at Dad.

The fire-alarm bell rang out.

"Everyone's running out the emergency exit in the back!" Charlie yelled to us.

"You have to let her go, Rik!" Ms. Watson called out to him.

"No!" he shouted. "Veri! Veri, come on!"

"She has to do it herself!" Ms. Watson told him.

Just then my powers flung me so hard that I broke free from dad's grip, went flying across the room, and smashed into the gift table, knocking it down. The force of the impact was enough to break my power surge.

"Veri! Veri!" My dad lifted me out of the pile of presents.

Dad looked me over as Ms. Watson did a more professional check of my eyes.

"You're okay?" she asked as she wiped something purple off the side of my face.

"Think so, considering." I looked around and noticed the purple on her fingers. "What is that?"

Ms. Watson sniffed her finger. "Smells slightly indelible." She patted my head. "It's only ink. You crashed into the inkwell on the table. The fancy pen-and-ink set your dad wanted for everyone to sign the guest book—it must have spilled on you."

"Permanently purple?" I asked.

"No, it'll come off with some wipes I have in the car."

"Phew!" I looked around, suddenly noticing the quiet. "Wait, where's Mom?"

"She took off," Dad said with disgust as he peered out a window.

"Who could blame her?" I said, seeing the mess I'd made of the gift table. Then it hit me. "I ruined the wedding!"

"No, you didn't," Dad said instantly.

"I did." It was pretty obvious. All the guests were gone. The presents were smashed. They weren't married.

"Were you arguing with anyone?" Ms. Watson asked pointedly.

"Well, no."

"That's what caused this to happen to you. You didn't cause this," she said definitively.

I felt tears fall down my cheeks. "I'm still sorry. I can see why you don't want me around anymore."

"What?!" they chorused.

"You two have your thing now and I'm just Weirdy McGee over here, ruining weddings and alienating mothers. I mean, I took the cure without telling you because I wanted to be normal so that she'd like me. And then I could go live with her and you'd get what you wanted, too."

"What do you think we want?" Dad asked. "'Cause it's not to live without you. However you want to be. Powers or not."

"He's right. We're getting married to make a more stable home for you, Veronica," Ms. Watson explained.

"And also because of love," Dad reminded her.

"And also love," she echoed quickly, but squirmed when she said "love." Talking about emotions wasn't her forte, even if she felt them deeply.

I let out a long, slow breath. Finally something made sense. I had wanted my mother's approval so badly that I hadn't been seeing what was true anymore. There wasn't a "normal" that would suddenly make everything okay. And it wasn't fair that she tried to make me think that being away from my dad would be good for me, let alone normal. If anything, I was getting the feeling that what was normal was going to change a lot in my life, and I wanted people around me who loved me and took care of me no matter what that normal looked like. For instance, me melted into a puddle on the floor.

"I love you guys. And I want to stay at home, so I'm really glad that's okay."

"Of course that's okay." Dad hugged me. "That will always be okay!"

"And we can talk about taking the cure. At the end of the day, though, it's up to you," Ms. Watson said. "We just want to be part of your decision, if that's something you really want."

"I don't know anymore," I told her.

She smiled. "You don't have to know right now."

"Yeah," Dad said, helping me up. "We still have a party to get to."

I wiped my eyes and looked at him. "We're still going to have the reception?"

"There's food. There's a karaoke machine. Nothing could keep me away." He gave me a big smile.

"We should go tell everyone. They're still in the parking lot," Ms. Watson said, touching Dad's elbow.

Dad looked at me.

"I'll be fine. The cavalry has arrived." I nodded toward the door. Both Betsy and Charlie were waiting there anxiously. "All clear," I told them.

"Not a hair out of place," Charlie joked when the three of us were alone.

"That was . . ." Betsy was at a loss for words.

"Yeah. Sometimes the powers are big."

"Did it hurt when you Hulk-smashed the table?"

"No. That was surprisingly fine. The powers themselves don't ever hurt me. Just make life really stupid difficult sometimes."

"After that, I can see why you wouldn't want them," Betsy said.

"But they're amazing! It's like every day is a surprise adventure!" Charlie blurted out. Then both he and Betsy clammed up, realizing they were in close proximity again.

"Uh, Charlie, can you guys help me get what's left of these presents in the car?" I asked. "Maybe, Betsy, you can find Lizzie and Dean? See how that's going?"

"You mean make sure they didn't catch anything incriminating on video?"

"Yep."

Charlie and I hauled the somewhat smashed wedding presents and put them in the trunk of Ms. Watson's car.

"Do they get to keep the presents? They didn't get married," Charlie wondered.

"That's a good point." I sighed. "I feel like such a jerk. When does it stop, Charlie?"

"You know how I feel, but you can stop it if it's what you want. The gummy will set you free." He tried to pick up one end of the portrait, but it was too unwieldy. "Here, grab that end."

I did but almost dropped it when I saw what I'd done.

"Oh no! Charlie! Look!"

He craned his neck around to see. In my stupidpower

frenzy I had smashed into the portrait while I was covered in purple ink.

"No way! It's you!" Charlie marveled.

"It's me?!"

"Look the right way. From my side," he instructed. "It's the perfect outline of your noggin and face!"

I tilted my head to the side and, indeed, there was stupid little me.

"I ruined it."

"Improved," Charlie said.

On the ride to the reception, I couldn't bear to tell Dad and Ms. Watson what had happened to the portrait. They had been through enough for one day and it showed. They weren't really speaking in the car and it seemed pretty tense. Once things had settled down, they had probably realized how I had actually ruined the day. They were totally mad at me.

⋆ ✳ ⋆

By the time we got to the club, I was completely sure that I was their least favorite person. They both got out of the car in a huff. I sat there for a second waiting for them to go inside, but they didn't. They just stood in front of the car looking at me. Might as well face the music.

"Tell her," Ms. Watson said firmly to Dad.

"Tell me what?"

Dad groaned, reached into his breast pocket, and pulled out a small sandwich bag containing one gummy bear.

I patted my pockets. Empty.

"You pinched my bear?! How did you even know?"

"Suspicious mind plus educated guess." He shrugged.

"But now?" Ms. Watson led him.

"But now I'm giving it back to you." He walked toward me and put it in my hand.

"Y-you want me to take it?" I was so confused. "Do you want me to go live with my mother?"

"Oh, one hundred percent no!" he said. "I want to keep you forever. *How*ever."

"But?" Ms. Watson said again.

"But that needs to be your decision." He gulped. "If you want this 'normal life' you keep talking about, then you should have it. There is nothing normal about us, Veri. Nothing normal about our life or our situation. But that doesn't mean it isn't good. In fact, it's what makes us our own family. It's what makes us *us*."

The door to the club swung open and the sounds of many people partying flooded out.

"We'll see you inside," Ms. Watson said, gently guiding my dad through the door.

Well, that was heavy.

"Cherry Veri Gumdrops McGee!"

"Hey, Ted," I said without turning around. It was very obvious it was him.

"We were right. That was a pretty epic wedding."

"Is a wedding without a wedding still a wedding?" I asked him in the most cryptic way I could.

"I think you just blew my mind!" He gasped.

"Don't say I never did anything for you," I teased.

"Oh! Oh! I was supposed to tell you something. From our *mutual acquaintance.*"

"You mean my mother."

"She said that she's ready to try again. She just needs . . ." Ted searched his mind trying to remember. "She just needs you to have 'the proof' and understand that you'll be sharing a room with Ignacio and, uh, Elvis."

The door swung open again, casting a warm light on us. Inside I could hear my dad laughing. After everything that happened today. After everything I ruined on his special day, my dad was laughing. There were no mental check lists. No demands.

"Do you want me to tell her anything?" Ted interrupted my train of thought.

"Uh, no," I said, still thinking about things. "You better get inside before all the food is gone," I warned him.

"Are you just chilling out here with your lonely gummy bear?"

I laughed. "Yeah."

Ted waved me off and headed inside, but I wasn't quite done.

"Actually, Ted!" I called after him. "Could you give her this? Tell her it's the only thing I'm going to share with her." I handed him the gummy bear baggie.

"This is very mysterious," he said with an approving smile.

"I'll see you inside, okay?"

He went in and left me alone in the cool autumn air.

"Woo!" I shouted. I felt amazing. A swell of happiness and love filled me, then popped out of me in the shape of my old friends the cutesy, giggling cartoon hearts. They all floated down and rested on the car like they were the perfect wedding decorations. Yep. I felt pretty darn amazing.

Well, amazing about almost everything. There was a rift I needed to close. I needed to be a bridge. Not in a literal sense, even though, since I had just decided I was keeping my powers, it was totally possible.

Inside the club I quickly spotted Charlie and Betsy. On opposite sides of the room, of course. They both looked pretty morose, which must have been really hard considering the ridiculously hilarious sight of my dad singing "Hungry Like the Wolf" onstage.

I grabbed three flutes of sparkling apple juice. I'd been so excited to have it! It looked so fancy! Anyway, it was an integral part of my plan. They were awkward to hold. Some would even say it was foolish to hold all three at once while you were trying to traverse a dance floor of middle-aged peeps rocking out to a giant man trying to sing soprano.

They would be right.

I had almost made it off the dance floor when I put on the most theatrics. I wobbled and added a few "Whoa!"s to really sell it. Before I could count to five, Betsy and Charlie had left their opposite corners to help.

"Oh, thanks!" I said as I handed each of them a flute.

Charlie started to chug his out of nervousness.

"Whoa, slow down," I told him. "I want to make a toast."

Charlie spit what was left in his mouth back into the glass.

Unexpectedly, Betsy let out a snort. "Charlie man, sometimes you are so . . . Charlie."

"Quick thinking with turning up the music, Bets," Charlie complimented her. "No one heard the fight."

"I speak Fist Face's language, what can I say?"

We all laughed.

"That's actually what my toast is about," I told them.

"Fist Face will be so pleased!" Charlie joked.

"I wanted to thank the both of you for always having my back."

"Even when you stage something like this?" Betsy pointed to her glass.

"How did you know?" I asked, but she rolled her eyes at me. "So, I wanted to tell you that I plan on being just as back-having for you two as you have been for me. From here on out. Three amigos." I raised my glass.

"Three musketeers." Betsy raised her drink.

"Three . . ." Charlie thought. ". . . Blind mice?"

We clinked glasses and cheered.

"Veronica, can I borrow you for a moment?" Ms. Watson tapped on my shoulder.

"Uh, sure. Everyone all right here?" I asked Betsy and Charlie.

"I promise I won't write any love notes while you're gone."

"Oh! Too soon!" Betsy laughed and smacked Charlie playfully on the back.

I giggled and followed Ms. Watson to a (reasonably) quiet corner.

"There are just a few things I feel we should set straight," she said very seriously.

"Oh, um, okay."

She exhaled sharply before continuing. "I did go speak with your mother. I knew that you were in contact with her and I had done my best to stay out of it, but I had a moment of poor judgment. I'm sorry I interfered."

"You knew I was talking to her the whole time?"

"I had my suspicions after you wanted to invite her, yes. And we only had thirty-seven blank invites instead of the thirty-eight we should have had."

"It's okay, Ms. Watson. I mean, compared to how my

dad would have reacted? He would have flipped out as soon as he knew."

"Well, the books on parenting I've read had very mixed opinions—"

"Why have you been reading books on parenting?" I gasped. "Are you pregnant?!"

"No! No!" She looked absolutely panicked. "No!"

We caught each other's eyes and laughed.

She continued, "I've been reading them because I am very eager to be *your* parent, Veronica."

"You read them for me?"

"I want to be a good parent, but not just that." She steeled herself. "I really do care about you."

Tears rose to my eyes, and my chin started to quiver. That was the nicest, most unexpected thing she could have said, but suddenly it all made sense: the weird up-and-down robot Ms. Watson, her wanting to talk to me about Charlie, and now finding out that she was dogging my mother to keep me safe. Wow. I couldn't control myself. I pulled Ms. Watson into the biggest bear hug I could possibly give her.

She let out a smooshed laugh and added, "Plus, I wanted to thank you—I think I'm going to get the city hall wedding I always wanted."

"I'm so gonna call you Mom!" I said.

"Let's take it one step at a time," she cautioned.

"Mommy? Do you prefer Mama?" I teased as I let go of her.

"I can't wait to ground you," she kidded.

"What! Ms. Watson, you made a joke!" I hugged her again.

"It is a special occasion," she said.

"Where are my ladies at?!" Dad bellowed from the stage.

"Hide me, please," Ms. Watson begged as I dragged her to the stage.

There was only one reasonable thing left to do: sing some karaoke.

EPILOGUE

One week later . . .

It wasn't every day that your dad got married to your guidance counselor. Even on days it was planned, it sometimes didn't happen. But it finally had.

"Should we flip a coin to see who carries who over the threshold?" I asked.

"Is that another antiquated marriage tradition?" Ms. Watson asked me.

"Yep."

She raised an eyebrow at Dad. "The only way you're carrying me anywhere is if you hobble me first."

Dad laughed. "Duly noted. Veri, why don't you do the

honors before we freeze out here?" He handed me the house keys.

"Sure!" I unlocked and whipped open the front door. "Welcome home Mr. and Mrs. Both Keeping Their Original Last Names!"

Above the fireplace hung the portrait I had drawn for them. Smooshed in there with them was the perfect outline of the face of yours truly in purple ink. The wedding portrait was now a family portrait.

As Ms. Watson put on some quiet classical tunes and Dad whipped up two celebratory cocktails and one delicious mocktail, I stared at the portrait for a minute.

"I think it's time we talk about getting me my own set of keys," a familiar, British-ish voice came from the doorway.

"What are you doing here?" I asked Charlie as I skipped to meet him.

"I was invited to a small gathering of all the coolest people. Oh, and Betsy's here, too," he joked.

"Hey," Betsy said, shutting the door behind her.

Dad popped his head out of the kitchen door. "Greetings!"

"Hi, Bets!" I said as I looked to Dad, happily surprised.

"We couldn't keep Chuck away from a family function with a stick," Dad said, then added playfully, "but we actually *wanted* Betsy to come." Dad mussed Charlie's hair. "Give me a hand with the lemons," he said, motioning for Charlie to join him back in the kitchen.

"What can we do?" I asked after him.

"Just chill out."

"Well then, come on, Bets, let's 'chill out.'"

Betsy and I went into the living room and sat on the sofa.

"You know you could start your own type of art," Betsy said.

"What?"

She pointed at the portrait. "Using your powers. Like, that is some pretty modern, experimental art right there."

"You think it's good like that?"

She sighed. "It's freaking perfect."

I couldn't help but giggle. A year ago I couldn't have imagined sitting in my living room with Betsy talking about art. Let alone having her compliment mine. If I really thought about it, my powers were what had brought Betsy and me together. What had made us friends. Actually, now that I really, *really* thought about it, they were also the reason I had Ms. Watson in my life now, too.

"It is perfect," I finally agreed. "Thank you."

We gave each other a quick smile.

"So," I said in a quieter tone, "seems like things are okay with you and Charlie?"

She nodded. "Thankfully, he finally figured it out."

"Figured what out?"

She looked at me, confused for a moment. Then it was like a switch flipped in her head. "Oh. You don't get it either."

"Get what?!" My whisper was in danger of becoming a shout.

"I hope everyone is thirsty!" My dad, Ms. Watson, and Charlie were about to come into the room.

"What don't I get?!" I asked Betsy again, frantically.

Bup-Bup-Bup-Buhh! Charlie imitated the sound of fanfare as the trio arrived with the drinks.

I tried to mentally force Betsy to answer, but she was looking at Charlie sheepishly as he carried over a tray of three lemony-looking cocktails in beer mugs with twirled bendy straws and fruit skewers.

"Bets!" I whispered.

She leaned over and whispered in my ear. "Even if I liked Charlie, I'd always come in second, dummy. It will always be you." Betsy snapped back up to accept a fruity consumable from Charlie. He then offered one to me.

"Cheers," he said.

His hand touched mine as I took the glass from him. Suddenly, what Betsy had said sunk in.

Whoosh! Tip-tip-tip-tip!

In an instant, all the lights went out, the fireplace was filled with a beautiful roaring fire, and every candle in the room lit up. It was like magic!

Or it was something else. Everyone looked at me.

It was still pretty magical, though.

I raised my glass. "To something super!"

"To something super!" everyone repeated.

THE END

P.S. Turns out, Ms. Watson lived in a cute little duplex. Sadly, there were no skulls, figurines, or roommates named Steve. Despite trying really hard, the only odd thing I found when we were helping her move out was an entire drawer filled to the brim with flower seed packets. Like, hundreds of them. At least now we have a project for next summer.

Acknowledgments

All the thanks to:

John Morgan, Erin Stein, and Weslie Turner at Imprint. Work shouldn't be this fun! Eternally grateful for the opportunity and support.

Bernadette Baker-Baughman. You are just the best ever.

The Nuhfer Clan, Paul, and Einstein. Beautiful weirdos each one.

About the Author

Heather Nuhfer was born near the Allegheny Mountains, where, from the safety of her bedroom, she wrote stories featuring her own monsters.

While working at the Jim Henson Company, Heather finally met many creatures face-to-face, including the lovable characters of Fraggle Rock. Heather scripted the lead story in Henson's Harvey Award–nominated Fraggle Rock graphic novel series, and she is the author of several My Little Pony: Friendship Is Magic graphic novels. She has also penned stories for *Wonder Woman*, *Teen Titans GO!*, *The Simpsons*, *Scooby Doo*, and *Monster High*, and Hasbro's *Littlest Pet Shop*. My So-Called Superpowers is her first series of prose novels.

When she isn't writing, Heather loves to knit while watching bad 1990s action movies with her beloved furbaby, Einstein.